BOUND BLOOD

FOREVER BOUND
BOOK TWO

TALA MOORE

EVA KINGSLEY

CONTENTS

PROLOGUE

BREC

They say your first memory is the foundation of how you'll live your life, and in my case, they were right. I don't know how old I was, but I know I was helpless to do anything to stop what was happening.

I saw my mother entangled in the arms of a shadow, blood dripping from her neck. I remember her curly blonde hair being stained red. I remember the smile on her lips as she embraced the shadow, and I remember how pale she went before she looked at me the last time with her lifeless blue eyes.

I knew I was crying as the shadow set her on the ground, but it was like I wasn't myself. More shadows formed around me as I became angry for the first time, and the shadow that had killed my mother materialized into the man I would love and loathe for the rest of my existence.

"Brec, my son, I'm so sorry..." He picked me up as he cried, carrying me away from my mother for the last time. "I truly thought it was her. I thought she would come back to me... I'll never forgive myself..."

People swarmed into our little cabin in the woods and took my mother out the back door. The man who called me son walked me to a horse-drawn carriage and put me in the arms of a young man.

"This is Adam, your brother. Adam? You must look after Brec. I have to find your mother again. I can't stop, I'm sorry my son... I can't live without her anymore..."

Adam clutched me. We were both crying now as our father turned to shadow and disappeared into the ether. I looked up into the face of the boy who held me; black hair like me, steel-gray eyes like me, but years more trauma in his life than I had yet to face.

"It will be okay, Brec, there are people who will look after us. We'll be fine without Father. I should know."

He hugged me close, and I knew then that this boy would be my primary source of comfort for the rest of my life.

The carriage rumbled away and I screamed and reached for my mother in our house, but Adam held me back. I cried and cried until I passed out from exhaustion, and when I woke again, Adam was carrying me inside the doors of an enormous castle. Servants offered to take me, but Adam ignored them. He walked through monstrous stone corridors until we got to a great room with a huge bed.

All around the room were toys, old toys and new toys, toys I could have never imagined. There was even a small copy of the castle for a playhouse. Adam set me down but took me by the hand and helped me walk to the little replica. He took me inside and we sat on pillows.

"This is my favorite spot, no one bothers me here. When you're hungry I'll go get us blood, okay? How did your mom feed you?" I motioned to his wrist, I didn't want to talk yet. "She fed you herself? So did my mom...before. I'll get a wet nurse for you until you can drink from a cup like me. Don't worry, they love us here. They want to feed us. It will be okay, little brother."

We slept in the playhouse every night for months, until Father brought back another human woman and fell into the throes of passion again. My nurse was a sweet maiden, mother to her own human children, and we all grew up together. I got my chance to be the big brother soon after, and I watched another mother die and our father disappear again.

One night, I must have been about ten, I gathered my brothers in the playhouse. Most of us were too big to be in there now, but Adam held little Corbett as he cried, covered in his mother's blood as our father screamed somewhere in the castle.

I frowned, looking at all my brothers. "I hope I never find my Forever Bound, not ever."

They all nodded. None of us wanted to live like this, fathering children and murdering their mothers in hopes of finding a reincarnated mate.

It wasn't worth it, and I swore that day that I would never seek out a woman, ever.

CHAPTER 1
XANTHE

S itting in front of a wall of security cameras, I twist my wild, curly blonde hair into a messy bun. As usual, I'm cross legged in my office chair, half the time spinning in circles and the other half of the time ready to bust out of the office with my gun ready. No one's gonna hurt my babies, not while I worked security for the children's wing of the hospital.

Right now, I'm chewing on a pencil and scrolling on my phone. So many emails from doctors... *Delete*. Doesn't matter. I already know everything they've got to say. And I don't want to hear it.

"You keep chewing on pencils, you'll get lead poisoning." I roll my eyes at Doug and stop spinning my chair with a shoe on the control panel. "And you're supposed to be wearing your non-slip security provided shoes, not pink converse high tops."

"You worry too much, my friend. Besides, it won't be this pencil that takes me out!"

We both laugh and I spin in the chair again. Doug is like an uncle to me, twice my age and rotund in the middle. I stand and stretch and he rolls his eyes this time.

"I'm pretty sure your uniform is two sizes too small as well."

I grin, turning to look at my butt. "But I make it look sooo good!" I wiggle my eyebrows at him and lean over the control panel. "Looks quiet today, huh? No weirdos, no running nurses, no—"

"You did *not* just say the Q word!" Doug snaps at me and slaps his forehead. As if on cue, two thugs come in the emergency room entrance toting guns and a bleeding buddy. "You jinxed us!"

Doug gets up and shakes his head at me, but I'm grinning ear to ear. Finally, some excitement. Fist bumping, we both take off running for the ER.

"You know, if you make that uniform look any better, we won't even have to tackle these guys. They're just gonna fall over drooling," he jokes as we skid around the corner and I hit a wall.

Non-slip shoes really would have been better today.

"Oh come on, you know I don't care about that stuff!" I chuckle and barely avoid running into a doctor.

"Slow down, Xanthe, this is a hospital, not a race track!" the doctor yells.

The alarms start to sound as a voice comes over the speaker, *code black, everyone shelter in place.*

"Ok, I'll let you handle the code black in the emergency room, then?" I challenge him.

Doug and I laugh as we turn the last corner to see the thugs waving their guns at the sick people and doctors alike.

I saunter in as if this isn't a life or death situation. "Whew! Gentlemen, you really shouldn't make a girl run this early in the morning!" I wave my face, hating that my heart is actually thumping after such a short sprint. "Now, are we gonna put the guns down or do I get to put you down?" I raise an eyebrow at them.

Dying by a bullet saving a hospital is the best way I can think to go.

One of the thugs tilts his gun to the side and aims it at my heart, right as Doug plows into him from the side.

"Yes! Nailed him!" I leap at the second thug, swinging around his neck and grappling him from the back. "Down, boy!" I shout at him as I slowly cut off his oxygen supply with my arm around his neck.

As soon as he passes out, I release him and cuff him with a flourish.

"You can cuff me like that any time!" the doctor I nearly ran into says as I straddle the thug's back.

"In your dreams, lover boy!" I wink at him and hand off the thugs to the sheriffs who arrive late, as usual. "Now buddy, what did we learn today?" I grip the thug's chin and make him look at his friend as he's wheeled to the emergency room. "Did we learn you catch more flies with honey than with bullets?" He glares at me and I pat his face. "Take him away, boys!" I wave at the officers and look at Doug, who's got his hands on his knees as he tries to catch his breath.

"Where do you get the energy, Xanthe? Where can I get some?" He gasps for breath and I just laugh. He looks over my shoulder as Doctor Never-gets-the-hint comes up behind me and puts his hand on my hip.

I smile sweetly at him. "Did you see how I took down that tattooed battle-scarred thug? You wanna see how much easier it is for me to remove your hand, or will you stop touching me on your own?"

His hand is off me before I blink. "Come on, Xanthe, when are you gonna let me take you out for dinner?" he pouts.

"Doug, are pigs flying outside?" I ask over my shoulder.

Doug grins and shakes his head, and the doctor's face goes red with fury.

"Not today, doc!" I smile and turn on a heel, taking Doug's arm and walking him back up the hallway.

"Am I the only man who isn't a leper to you, Xanthe?" Doug chuckles. "Just this week alone I've seen you turn down doctors, nurses, even janitors. Male and female alike! I think Grace just wanted a friend and you still turned her down! It's criminal to look as good as you do and have no one in your life, girl."

I lean my head on Doug's shoulder and sigh. "Oh, Doug, you're the only friend I need."

He pats my hand on his arm and stops walking to look at me seriously. "You can't spend your whole life pushing everyone away, Xanthe."

I smile up at him, honestly trying to listen. He doesn't know anything, no one does. I made sure my doctors were at an unconnected hospital, my records private. Thank you, HIPAA. I zone out as Doug goes into the same speech as always. How important it is to have friends since I have no family.

Internally, I roll my eyes. If only he knew...

I catch a flicker of movement from the corner of my eye. In the dimly lit hallway...is there someone standing there? I try to focus and the shadow moves, disappearing down another hall. Am I hallucinating? I rub my eyes and then pat Doug on the shoulder.

"I have to run to the bathroom. Be right back, bud."

As I walk away, he walks back to the security room. I don't actually have to pee, I need to make sure I'm not going insane.

I turn around the corner where the shadow went and see it again. The lights are flickering in this part of the hospital, and I can't decide if I'm looking at a man or something else. It disappears again and I follow. Finally, in the basement, the shadow enters the morgue.

I sneak in, quiet as I can, and watch the shadow solidify into a man as he slips inside the walk-in refrigerated unit. I pull my gun from its holster. I don't know what this shadow man wants with the cold blood storage but he's not gonna get it, not in my hospital! I swing the door open and stop it with my foot, aiming the gun.

"Stop right there!" I shout.

The man freezes. He's in a long black trench coat, wearing a fedora. He turns around slowly and my heart stops. It takes everything in me not to clutch my chest as I hold my gun steady. He's got a bag to his mouth, blood dripping down his chin, and he hisses at me with long fangs. I step forward and the door closes behind me, clicks.

Locks.

I stare into a pair of steel gray eyes, trying to force my heart to start beating right as my vision blurs, and fire as he lunges at me. The blast of the gun in such a small space nearly ruptures my eardrums and I flinch back from his attack. He pins me to the fridge door and raises me off the ground by my neck.

The bullet grazed his cheek, I'd missed, but to my astonishment it heals right in front of my eyes.

Vampire....

He roars in my face, specks of blood splattering me.

CHAPTER 2
BREC

The woman who found me will be an easy kill, I could snap her neck like I'm flicking a fly. Her useless existence means nothing to me. Roaring in her face, I savor the fear in her eyes. She should never have followed me.

Yet, I have to will my nails to turn into talons. I have to tighten my gut as I prepare myself for what I must do. Turns out, that hesitation is all she needs.

I bare my teeth, ready to drain her, but the fear has already dissolved from her eyes. I expect anger, for her to turn into a wildcat fighting for her life, but her mouth softens as she studies me with fascination.

"A vampire, huh?" She runs her hands up my arms. "Surely you're not hungry after that little snack."

I drop her, completely shocked.

She laughs! She actually laughs. She's supposed to be terrified, trembling in fear! I turn my back to her and clench my fists. It's almost like she sees into my soul and knows I've never been a killer.

I glare at her over my shoulder as she leans against the door and rubs her neck. Something about her seems familiar, the wild blonde curls, the ocean blue eyes. She smiles at me. Seriously, she's smiling at me? Her pink lips over her perfect white teeth stir something in me. I turn away again, taking off my hat and running my hand through my short black hair. I'm going to have to compel her, make her forget this ever happened. Instill her with a deep burning fear of shadows and men in long coats.

I turn and face her, trapping her against the fridge door and stare deeply into her eyes. "You will not remember this meeting. You will forget everything except for an unshakable fear of this place and shadows you don't understand. You will not recognize me if you see me again, you will be too afraid to approach me and run the other way."

To my utter amazement, she giggles. "You have beautiful eyes, by the way."

I bare my fangs in her face. She puts her hands on her hips and looks up at me without an ounce of fear in those aquamarine eyes.

"You realize we're locked in here, right? I can't just let you drink any more of this blood either, there are people here depending on it." She flips her blonde hair over her shoulder, suddenly looking all business. "So hands off the merchandise! And stop looking at me like that, if you're gonna eat me, just do it already."

She snatches the blood bag out of my hand and ducks under my arm, walking away from me fearlessly as she examines the bag to see if it can be saved. I can't help it, my jaw drops, she just ignored my heaviest glamor. I turn and step towards her as she faces away from me.

If I can't glamor her, I'll have to drain her.

"Well shit, I guess it's already contaminated. Even a monster has to eat, right?"

She holds the bag out to me and I step back quickly. I have to get out of here, away from this weird woman. I try to open the door. It doesn't budge. I punch the door, leaving a fist sized dent in it.

"Wow, damage to hospital property, too? When they come down here for blood for that thug upstairs, I'm totally handing you over to the authorities. Why don't you just put your hands behind your back willingly so I don't have to fight you? Deal?" She reaches for handcuffs, and her face goes pale when she doesn't find them. She swears under her breath and grabs the tubing around the blood bag with both hands, ready to tie me up if she has to.

I lean against the door and glower down at her menacingly; I'm a good two feet taller than her, a vampire, and she knows her gun is useless. Does she really think some plastic tubing is going to prevent me from escaping?

"Take your best shot, sunshine!" I scowl and turn around, trying to find any weaknesses this fridge might have. She yells something unintelligible and collides with my back.

I look at her over my shoulder as she tries to grapple me and choke me. I decide to humor her and let her wrap the tubing around my throat. I stand patiently as she realizes I don't need to breathe. With one hand I grab the back of her collar and pull her over my head, hanging her upside down by her ankle.

"Are you done yet?" I smirk at her as her face goes red with embarrassment.

"I'm just doing my job, now will you please stop being so preternaturally strong and let me arrest you?"

She smiles and I'm tempted to drop the foolish human on her head. I set her down gently, and she hops to her feet like a cat ready to go again.

"What's it gonna take? I don't think I'll find a cross in here. Hmmm..." She meanders around the room and puts her hand on one of the wooden shelves holding all manner of cold storage medical supplies. "Wooden stake? I'm sure if I piss you off enough, I can get you to break this shelf for me."

"Won't work, kitten." I lean back against the door, surrendering to be trapped with this tiny human. I call her kitten because her tiny ineffectual attacks are about as strong as a newborn cat trying to roar.

I watch her as she walks around, checking all the bottles and supplies. She fills that uniform better than any human I've seen; her ass is toned and perfectly round, her body strong. She must exercise regularly. I try to shake myself to attention, the way her body looks doesn't matter one bit, but when she puts her hands on her hips and glances at me over her shoulder, it makes my heart flutter for the first time I can remember.

Unwillingly, I imagine the buttons on her uniform bursting open and her large breasts being exposed, and I get hard almost instantly. I shake my head and push off the door, stalking towards her. I've never killed an innocent human, but there's a first for everything. This human vexes me, and I think it's time she's no longer a distraction.

"Ah ha! Colloidal silver!" She turns to me, victorious, holding a vial of silver fluid up in her hand. I flinch back, an uncontrollable reflex, and her jaw drops. "Ooooh, so this little vial of silver scares the big bad vampire?"

She grabs a needle and draws some out of the vial, walking towards me with an evil grin on her heart-shaped perfect face... My cock twitches. What is happening to me? There's nothing remotely sexy about being threatened with silver.

I let her push me back against a wall, holding the needle to my chin, and she unconsciously presses her body against me as she tries to pin my arms behind me with one hand. I scowl down at her as I realize she smells like sunshine and flowers, her skin tan like caramel. The way her hips sway as she struggles ineffectually to move my arms is transfixing.

With one quick move, I hook my arm around her waist and pin her against the wall. She instinctively wraps her legs around my waist and tries to push the needle into my neck, but it doesn't even prick the skin. I grin at her, baring my fangs and I grab the needle out of her hand and smash it on the floor.

With her body pressed against mine, she can't move, and I feel a surge of powerful control as she has the smarts to look scared. The fear in her eyes is making me feel drunk on power. I squeeze her wrists a little tighter and she yelps. Good, she's finally realizing what she's up against. That she's in mortal danger.

Out of nowhere, her expression flashes from scared to seductive. Surely not... But when she locks eyes with me again, she looks at me through her dark lashes and moves a little, as if testing all the places we touch. She bites her lip, her breathing getting heavy. Her chest rises and falls suggestively and I can't help but to look down at her cleavage.

"What are you doing?" I ask as I try to set her down,

Her feet touch the ground, but her eyes don't leave my mouth. There's a secretive little smile on her lips as she stands on her tiptoes and pulls me down by my collar, forcing my lips to hers.

Too shocked to react and pull away, I stare at her. Her eyes close and she sighs as she kisses me. My cock twitches as if the sound is directly connected to it. I'm speechless. Motionless. I've never felt a kiss before, and the warm softness of her mouth is making me absolutely crazy. Her tongue darts out, teasing the seam of my lips.

Finally able to react, I push her back firmly against the wall and pry her hands off my collar and pin them to the wall above her head. She smiles, her eyes heavy and her mouth parted. She licks her upper lip and I feel like I'm under a siren's curse. I lean in, unable to resist the way she looks at me, brushing her lips with mine. Heat explodes through me when she moans.

This human is strange, more strange than I could have ever imagined a human to be. Most would cower in my presence, screaming and trying to escape, but this confusing, delectable one? She lifts a leg and hooks it around my hips.

All thought escapes my mind as I feel her heat against my pants. I grip her thigh and press against her waist with my own. Her eyes ignite with passion and she grinds against me. There are so many new sensations at once that I lose control.

My mouth crushes against hers and the whole world seems to disappear.

CHAPTER 3
XANTHE

What am I doing... What am I doing?

The vampire has me pinned, I can feel his cock hard between my legs. His kisses are wild and rough, like he doesn't know what he's doing, and it's making me absolutely feral. This is crazy, even for me, but I grind my hips against his hard length and he growls into my mouth. I gasp, and his tongue slips in.

The moment he invades me, I'm lost. I don't care. I'm glad I've decided I'm going to live my life as if there's no tomorrow.

I play with his tongue with mine and he tastes like blood and whiskey, iron and silk. I grind harder against his cock, the friction of our pants rubbing together bringing me way too close, too fast. He's getting better at kissing, braver, his tongue ventures deeper into my mouth, his free hand exploring my body. He pulls my shirt out of my pants and slips his hands up my back.

I'm shocked as he unclasped my bra—he doesn't seem like he's very experienced—but he did that without issue. His kisses move to my neck as his hand slips around, his thumb grazes my nipple as he lifts my bra over my breasts and I moan loudly. The only thing holding me to the wall now is his hips. I wrap my hands around his neck, stroking his face as he leans back and starts to lift my shirt. I'm grinding hard, looking into his eyes as he licks his fangs. I realize with a thrill of fear that I want to lick his fangs, too.

I pull him back to me, my tongue darting out and doing just that. His eyes darken, a wildness taking over him as he pulls me off the wall and holds me in the air. He tugs my hair, making me tilt my head to the side, and drags those long dangerous fangs down my neck as he rips my shirt to the side and bites my shoulder. I shiver with delight, clinging to him for dear life as my mind goes wild. Will he break the skin? Will he drink from me here and now? What a wonderful way to die, with a huge cock inside me and him drinking my blood.

He sets me down on top of a shelf, scattering medical supplies as if they don't cost an arm and a leg, and forces himself back between my legs. Now he's grinding his hips against me, and his cock feels outrageously huge. I stare into his almost silver eyes and realize I'm completely lost in the moment. I'm suddenly obsessed with him, like I need to fuck him or I'll die, and I start to unbutton my pants. He's too close to me, rubbing me too powerfully, that I can't get my pants down. I slip my hand inside the hem of my panties and moan as I touch my clit.

He leans back, watching, hooking his arms under my knees and tilting me back so I can get a better angle. With one hand I'm rubbing my hot wet cunt and with the other I'm rubbing his impossibly strong muscled arms. I want to see him naked, I need him inside me! I feel drunk on the sensation, drunk on him. He's got to be the sexiest man I've ever seen and by some miracle he's grinding that huge cock on me and not some model.

I come suddenly, hard and fast, and oh so embarrassing. I

feel my fluids cover my hand and soak through my pants, but I can't stop. I cling to him, riding the orgasm like I'm riding his hips. When I finally finish, he's looking at me in shock, and I gently push him away. He sets me down and rubs his stiff cock under his damp pants.

I'm flushed, breathless, embarrassed. My heart is hurting, but I can't tell him that. I redo my bra hastily and tuck my pants back in. "Well...that was...fun..." I smile up at him sheepishly, wondering what the hell just happened. There's only living once, and then there's completely forgetting everything else exists.

He glares at me hungrily, reaching out for me, and I'm about to sidestep, too overwhelmed by what just happened, when the door opens and a nurse rushes in. She reels back to find two people inside, but I rush past her. "Oh, thank god! I was about to freeze!"

Out in the corridor, I discover my vampire close behind. My vampire? I stifle a nervous laugh. "I should still arrest you, but given the circumstances..." I spin on my heel, striding to the elevator and pressing the button. The fucker had better reach the basement quick. "You damaged hospital property and stole a blood bag..."

Glancing over my shoulder, I find he's already beside me, close. Too close.

"I own this hospital," he snarls, and I blanch. He leans forward and puts his hand on my chin, closing my mouth and making me look up at him as he leans over me. "What's your name, kitten?" A slight smile cracks his hard, stern mouth for the first time and I go weak in the knees.

"My name? Oh...yeah, no thank you. Have a nice day, don't steal anymore blood...even if you do...own it..."

Ding.

I duck out from under his arm and into the elevator as soon

as it opens, pressing the button for the doors to close over and over as he watches me.

"You work in my hospital. I'll figure it out sooner or later," he says, and it feels almost like a threat.

The door closes, cutting off the sight of his broody sexiness, and I fall into a crouch with my hands on my head.

"What. The. Fuck. Xanthe?" I smack my head and stand, pacing the elevator.

I've slept with my share of men, but never the moment I met them! Something about him made me absolutely crazy, I couldn't help it! If I hadn't come...if I'd fought it...where would it have gone? Would I have let him fuck me on that wall? A shiver of pleasure runs through me and I almost stop the elevator. I reach in my pants, leaning against the wall.

He made me so wet... I rub myself, my clit is throbbing. Should I go back? Will he still be there? Pleasure climbs through me, pulsing in anticipation and I'm close to coming again when I fall to my knees, doubled over in pain.

A strangled whimper tumbles from my lips as my surroundings swim. My chest feels like it's exploding and imploding all at once. Darkness beckons with the promise of oblivion, and fighting it has me panting. I reach with shaky hands to my pocket and grab a small metal vial. I dump a tiny white pill out and put it under my tongue, trying to catch my breath. I stand slowly, trying to compose myself as the elevator door opens and I'm face to face with Doug.

"Where have you been? We've got a thief on the third floor and an addict in the ER. Which one do you want?" He looks me over, noting my flushed face and disheveled hair. "Xanthe, are you okay?"

I smile brilliantly, glad the meds work quickly, even as I wish they'd work quicker. "Peachy keen! I'll take the thief since

I'm already in the elevator." I press three and wave as the door closes and Doug narrows his eyes at me.

I let out a breath, willing my pulse to settle. I can tell he knows something, I'll have to think of a convincing lie before I get back. If he finds out I kissed a man let alone dry humped him until I came, I'll never hear the end of it.

If he finds out I have a couple of health issues I've failed to mention...

The door dings open and a small person collides with me, pill bottles scattering everywhere. "Well, that was easy!" I say as I pin the boy's arm behind his back and wrestle him to the ground. "Aren't you a little young to be stealing opioids, kid?" I smirk and grab a bottle, amoxicillin.

I take a better look at the boy, he's young and filthy, likely homeless. The medicine he has is for fighting infection, another bottle is for nausea.

I loosen my grip, compassion softening my resolve, and his elbow flies back and nails me in the nose. I fall backward, blood trickling down my face as the kid scrambles to his feet and collects the pills. He looks at me in disgust before he escapes as the doors conveniently open.

I lay on the ground, cursing internally at my own stupidity, then groan when I see my vampire in the hallway with his arms folded sternly over his chest.

"You've got to be kidding me," I mutter.

He stops the elevator and walks in, not bothering to chase the boy, instead helping me to my feet as the door closes behind him. "You just took on a vampire, but you can't stop some street rat?" he laughs and I glare at him.

"He caught me off guard!" I lie, avoiding eye contact.

He rolls his eyes and takes a silk handkerchief out of his pocket and gently wipes my face. "Lucky, it's not broken." He taps my nose playfully. "But you've been a naughty kitten, I should hold you responsible for the losses."

"And I should have you arrested for stealing something worth way more than antibiotics!" I snap back, squaring up to him and ready to fight.

"Tell you what, kitten, you tell me your name and I won't call security." He smirks at his own joke and puts the handkerchief back in his pocket as soon as the blood stops.

"Xanthe," I say between clenched teeth and a hard glare.

"Xanthe...?" he asks.

"Xanthe NonYaBusiness!" I push past him and out of the elevator as soon as it opens, but he follows close behind.

"I only have to check employee records to find out your last name, Xanthe. Such an exotic name, where did you get it?" He takes off his trench coat and reveals a three-piece suit. He must have left his hat in the cold storage. Something about that inconvenience makes me giddy. He follows me closely and I can feel the heat rolling off of him.

"Ask the orphanage," I say over my shoulder, hoping the lie about being an orphan will make him stop asking. I stop as I get to the door of the security room. "Sorry, boss, only security is allowed in here." I wave and try to walk in the room, but he grabs my wrist and pulls me back.

"When do you get off work tonight?" he asks, looming over me menacingly. There's something soft in his eyes though, and I get the sense he has no idea how to flirt with a woman.

"Wouldn't you like to know!" I pull my hand from his and step through the door and lock it behind me. I stick my tongue out at him through the glass window and he glowers at me before he walks away. I turn on a heel and look right into the shocked face of Doug.

"Don't start!" I snap. "Just another man who won't take a hint."

Doug arches a brow at me and turns to face the security screens. "Sure looked like more than that in the elevator!" Doug smirks and sips his coffee. "But what do I know, I'm just an old man who's never been interested in a woman." He glances at me from the corner of his eye and I stomp my foot.

"You were spying on me?" I shriek, and he grins.

"There was no addict in the ER, I just wanted to see what you were up to. It's my job to look after everyone in this hospital. You do know he's not just a 'man' right? That's Brec Cadell, owner and CEO of the whole hospital."

I sit in my chair with a thud. Brec Cadell... Xanthe Cadell... *No Jesus, what the fuck!* I slap my head and spin in my chair. "I don't care if he's the long-lost prince of Egypt. He's not getting near me!"

Doug makes a sound in his throat that tells me he doesn't believe a word I'm saying. "With the kind of power that man has, Xanthe, you're lucky he let you get this far away from him. I've seen a love-struck man, and he's got it bad." He laughs and sips his coffee again.

"You're out of your mind, Doug. No one gets love struck after a meeting in an elevator." I pull a loose curl from my bun and twirl it around my finger, watching the screens.

Doug starts humming 'love is in the air' and I throw the orange I brought for lunch at his head. He ducks and spills his coffee all over his pants and I grin victoriously.

I'm not getting entangled with anyone, pantie-melting hot vampire or not.

CHAPTER 4

BREC

"Yes, Adam, I know..." I say, striding into the hospital the next day. There's a board meeting today that I can't miss, and I need to find my hat.

"We know it's real now, Brec. I want this for you, for all of you. Having your Forever Bound is like seeing color for the first time." Adam's voice drops in that way it does when he's talking about Kiera. "I'm telling you, her belly gets bigger every day and they're both so powerful already. Besides that, the Monroes will not honor their matriarch much longer. Doesn't matter that she's Kiera's mom, she'll do what she has to do to protect her sons. We need you all to find your women, or we have no chance."

I scowl at the elevator doors. Adam is out of his mind, it's love, not a Forever Bound bond. None of it is real.

"Are you listening, Brec?"

"Yes, Adam. I have a lot on my plate, you know," I growl over the phone and Adam laughs.

"Listen, you can't be so gruff and angry your entire existence. You're going to have to smile more than once a century if you want to attract a woman—"

"Adam, that's enough," I interrupt him, but Xanthe smiling at me flashes in my memories and I think about how she made me want to smile. "I have another call coming in, I'll call you back."

I hang up the phone without so much as a goodbye and enter the elevator. Between Adam and Father, they're not going to let this go. I have to think of something to get them off my back...

Maybe the morgue? I can say I found my Forever Bound as she was dying, oh well? I roll my eyes. That's just stupid. I think of Xanthe again and my cock gets hard against my will. I want to see her again, contrary to my feelings over all these centuries. She tasted like mint when I kissed her, and tasting her again is all I can think about. I adjust my pants, trying to hide the obvious hard on before the elevator opens on the top floor.

As I step through the door, a crazy idea hits me. A solution that will get Adam and Father off my back. A solution that doesn't mean sucking some poor woman dry while I watch the life drain from her eyes.

I crack a genuine smile and it hurts my face a little as I go back into the elevator to head to the security room. The moment the decision is made, there's a desperation in me to be near her, to smell her, to touch her. A desperation I'm not used to feeling. All my life, the only thing I've felt is hunger for blood and a sheer loathing of the Forever Bound lore. It occurs to me that maybe we could continue where we left off at the morgue. The thought thrills me, having never been interested in a woman I find the feeling unsettling yet impossible to resist.

When I get to the security there, I discover she's not inside, but I see her on one of the screens. She's walking through the pediatric ward, so I head there next. In the elevator again, I start to feel nervous. I've never felt like this before, yet all I can think about is what color her nipples are.

The door dings open and I walk into the pediatric ward. The smell of terminal illness hits me like a wave. Sickly blood, dying children. I mold my face into a scowl as I tell my heart this is how it has to be as I walk through the halls looking for Xanthe. I can smell her as I get closer, mint chewing gum and liquid sunshine. I round a corner and find her in a room, hanging paper flowers from the wall and talking animatedly to a little girl laying in the bed.

"We'll make this room an enchanted forest in no time!" she's saying.

She's drawn whiskers on her face and hops around like a bunny for the laughing little girl. The little girl giggles and draws my attention away; she's deathly sick, pale white and bald, her brown eyes sunken, but her laughter is full of life. I can smell her though, and she won't bless this earth with that smile much longer. For the first time, I start to understand Corbett's fascination with vampiric immortality. Why do we live forever, while children such as this die before they've lived?

I mentally shake myself. It doesn't matter. Humans die. We live on. It's best not to get attached.

I walk through the door and clear my throat. "Xanthe, when you're done here, I need to see you in my office," I announce, not looking at the little girl at all and trying to seem as menacing as I've been every day of my life until she tried to arrest me.

"Anyone who walks through that door has to be a magical being, or they can't enter the magical forest," the little girl says. "Xanthe's my angel, so what are you?" she asks, then coughs.

I look at her and she just smiles, not the least bit intimidated by my huge looming glare.

Xanthe sits on the bed next to the girl and whispers loudly, "You won't believe this, but he's a vampire!" I glare at her in utter disbelief, but she smiles up at me like the devious little minx she is. "A very grumpy vampire!" she adds, and the little girl laughs.

"Hi mister vampire sir! I'm Mara!" She beams up at me and Xanthe stares daggers, warning me without words that I better be nice.

I'm tempted to turn on my heel and walk out. I'm too old for this kind of foolishness. But that would mean walking away from Xanthe. I wouldn't find out what color her nipples are...

I roll my eyes and take my jacket off, tossing it over a chair before walking up to her bed.

"I vant to suck your blood!" I snarl at the little girl, raising my hands up like a television vampire. "Blaaa bla bla!" I lunge at her playfully, and she shrieks with laughter and hides in Xanthe's chest.

Xanthe looks up at me and her eyes sparkle with unshed tears. She mouths 'thank you,' then squeals playfully. "Back, you fiend! Pick on someone your own size!"

I smile at her as she waves me away. "Someone like you?" I growl, put a knee on the bed and grab her wrist, kissing the inside of her palm and watching her squirm. She blushes and pulls her hand away, grabbing a nearby broom stick and waving it at me.

"I'm nowhere near your size! I'm just a tiny little human! Go fight a gargoyle!"

I round the bed, snatching the broom and pulling her against my chest. I bury my face in her neck, pushing her curls away as I kiss her neck while growling.

"Not my angel!" Mara gasps and kicks me.

I grunt and fall to my knees, releasing Xanthe and clutching my chest.

"Mara! You have beaten me! The great vampire falls to the hands...of a...child..." I say the last part through desperate gasps for air before I collapse on the hospital floor and pretend to die.

"Oh no!" Mara gasps, her breathing becoming labored. "Xanthe, you have to kiss him! Only true love can bring him back!"

"True love? I barely know the guy!" Xanthe laughs, but Mara's breathless now. "Okay, okay, I'll kiss him!" She falls to her knees and pulls me into her lap. "Oh, vampire, do not go into the light! I love you!" She pulls me close and kisses me chastely, but I grab her head and pull her down, kissing her thoroughly. Tasting her tongue again sets me on fire, and the way she looks at me when I pull back tells me she feels the same.

"You saved him, true love!" Mara gasps for breath and Xanthe gently pushes me away and stands up.

"Are you alright, sweet pea?" She gets a wet cloth and gently dabs the girl's forehead.

"Uh huh... I think I'm just tired now. Angel? When I die, will you promise to still love the vampire? You need someone..." Mara's eyes close and she falls asleep.

Xanthe tries to hide it but she wipes away tears before she waves me out of the room.

"Lung cancer," she says, taking a deep breath. "It's metastasized. She doesn't have long..." She squares her shoulders and turns to face me, all the security guard and none of the magical angel left on her face. "What did you need?" She rubs her neck where I kissed her, and her words trail off as she looks at the floor.

It feels like I'm alive, I actually had fun. I feel joy, I feel hope. After meeting Mara, the idea of spending more time with Xanthe is even more enthralling. "Is there somewhere around here where we can talk in private?"

She raises a brow at me, her pretty pink mouth smirking with curiosity. "Sure, follow me..." she says, and turns away.

I swear she's swaying her hips like that on purpose. I'm

paying so much attention to the way her ass moves that I forget my jacket in Mara's room. Xanthe leads me to a dark office without a window and ushers me inside. "Dr. Whitlam doesn't work Saturdays, didn't think the CEO would either. So what's up?"

I watch as Xanthe sits on the desk and crosses her legs and arms, looking at me expectantly. I swallow hard, fighting the urge to just kiss her instead of talk, but I force myself to take a seat in one of the guest chairs.

"Well, you know I'm a vampire, obviously." She nods, and I grip the handles of the chair. "What you don't know is that vampires have fated mates, like soul mates."

"I'm not your soulmate, Brec!" She laughs quietly and I shake my head.

"I know, I know. What I'm saying...what I'm asking...is if you would like to pretend. Would you be my Forever Bound? Just for a month, just long enough to convince my family that I've found one so they leave me alone."

"You've got to be kidding me!" She tries to stand and I leap up, putting my hands on her shoulders.

"How about just a week? Spend a week with me, meet my family. I'll pay you, price is not a concern of mine, just name it."

Xanthe goes quiet, her eyes assessing me. I wait, unsure of what that means, every muscle coiled. I'm not sure what I'm going to do if she says no.

She lets out a sigh, her face settling into an expression that tells me she's made a decision. It was quicker than I thought. Surely that can't be a good thing...

She pushes my hands off her shoulder and stands up, walking to the door. "Let me get this straight, the big scary vampire needs a little ol' me to pretend to be his lover?" She looks over her shoulder at me and locks the office door.

"That about sums it up...." I answer, growing nervous as she turns and walks slowly back to me.

"I don't want your money, Brec." She pushes her body against mine, her hand sliding down and rubbing my cock. I'm immediately rock hard and she smiles at me, a sense of power washing over her. "I don't do anything half assed, if I'm going to be your lover—even for a week—it's going to be real." She starts unbuttoning my pants and I'm filled with genuine terror.

I've never seen a woman naked, maybe at the bathhouses of old but never like this. Am I even ready?

"Are you serious? Here? Now?" I look over her shoulder and she sinks to her knees and pulls my cock out. She gasps and I flinch. "Is it too big? I'm sorry, I know it's bigger than most, you don't have to..."

I choke as she wraps her mouth around my length. I fall back, gripping the desk with all my strength. What is she doing? I've seen sex before but not this, never this. I groan, her tongue is swirling around the head of my cock as she sucks and moans.

I can't think straight, all that's going through my head is the crazy way her mouth feels on me. She gently eases my pants down to my ankles and one hand grips the base of my cock and the other massages my balls. It's too much. Too overwhelming. I groan and bite my own hand as I explode in her mouth, waves of pleasure coursing through me.

Her eyes go wide with surprise but she looks up and me and her gaze turns pure evil. She sucks harder, swallowing every drop of my seed, power and control rolling off her as I'm helpless in her mouth. All I can do is ride the ecstasy I never knew existed.

When I finally finish I'm trembling, weaker than I've ever felt, and feeling more vulnerable than when I was a child. She stands, a sly grin on her face as she starts unbuttoning her shirt.

Her nipples are a chocolate brown, a few shades darker than her skin.

"You're a virgin, aren't you?" she asks as she slips off her pants, revealing a dark patch of curls between her legs. So, she's not a natural blonde...my cock goes hard all over again.

I look at her, unable to speak. Her wide hips, her perfect huge perky breasts. Her nipples are hard, and as she unbuttons my shirt and presses her naked body against me, I come all over her stomach, groaning brokenly. Every nerve is alive in ways it shouldn't be inside a vampire body.

"Oh god, I am so sorry..." Mortified, I try to find something to clean her up, but she just rubs it on her skin and then licks it off her fingers.

"This is going to be more fun than I imagined..."

She grabs my cock softly and uses it to guide me around the desk to the office chair behind it. She pushes me down, and crawls onto my lap. Without any warning, she sits on my cock, and my life flashes before my eyes. I could die, right here in this moment, the sheer pleasure of her tightening around me has me out of my mind. I grip her hips desperately as she takes every inch of me inside her.

When she's sitting fully on my lap, the small gasp that leaves her perfect mouth makes me lose it again. I roar behind my gritted teeth, full of possessive victory and deep embarrassment. I fill her with my seed and watch it drip out of her and onto me.

She laughs, wrapping her arms around my neck and wiggling her hips. "We're gonna have to practice your stamina."

She gasps when I grab her hips and thrust hard up into her, her eyes going as wild as I feel. She arches her back, her tiptoes barely touching the ground, and rides me slowly with her eyes locked on mine.

CHAPTER 5
XANTHE

I start slow, causing very little friction as I pull him in and out of me. He's so fucking big... I've never had anyone even half as big. The way he fills me, I feel like I'm impaling myself. I'm rabid with need, and absolutely crazed when he comes inside me almost instantly. He looks totally bewildered, his eyes can't focus on anything. He throws his head back, his moans almost pleading for mercy. I grab his hand and put it on my lower back, and grab his other hand and have him squeeze my breast.

Grabbing his shoulders I lean back as far as I can, slowly increasing the pace. The way he looks at my body makes me feel so powerful, his cock inside me makes me feel pleasure like I never imagined. He grabs my hips suddenly, making me stop, and it seems like he's holding his breath.

"Brec? What's wrong?" I sit up, cradling his head against my breasts, and he groans and comes again.

"I am so fucking sorry..." he mutters, clinging to me hard so I can't look at him. At this point I have so much come inside me it's starting to drip on the floor.

"Brec..." I moan, tightening my pussy around him and

feeling him grow hard already. "Stop apologizing...your cum is so hot, it feels so good..." I rock against him, running my sharp nails up and down his back.

"You like the way it feels?" he growls, and his hands grow sharp claws that dig into my skin.

I moan; the danger, the claws, the monster fucking me...

"I fucking love the way everything about you feels!" I moan.

His cock jerks inside me, and he lifts me up and throws me on the desk with a bestial growl.

He lowers himself over me, one hand behind my head and the other on my breast and starts fucking me like a pro. I moan loudly, too loudly for the children's ward or for the hospital itself, for that matter. I try desperately to stay quiet but I can't, his cock is too big, too perfect. I grab his shoulders, biting my lip when he puts his hand over my mouth.

I'm shocked, my eyes go wide but he still fucks me as hard as before. "Moan as hard as you need to, kitten...don't hold back..."

I throw my arms over my head and lock my ankles around his back. Anchoring myself to the desk, I lift my hips off the table and match his thrusting stroke for stroke. His hand over my mouth muffles my sounds so I let myself go absolutely wild. Brec's eyes never leave me, one hand digging into the flesh of my thick thighs and the over gently but firmly muting my moans.

I've never felt pleasure this intense, and somewhere in the back of my mind I realize how long he's lasting now. He's focused on me, on my pleasure, he's watching which strokes make me moan and which I'm quiet on. He's studying me, learning me, my god I could get addicted to this! I grab his shoulders and pull him down to me, holding my breast up to his mouth.

"Lick... suck..." are the only words I can get out between

groans. He dives in eagerly, sucking vigorously and a bit too hard. "Careful.... Tender..."

He immediately softens, caressing me with his tongue and sucking so gently I feel as if I'm coming undone. I need to come so bad it hurts. I greedily put my hands between my legs and massage my own clit, moaning and arching.

Brec stands straight, watching my fingers like he's in a trance, studying what I'm doing before he snatches my hand away and sucks on my fingers. I watch as his eyes roll back in his head as he tastes me, and I squeal in delight when his thumb finds my clit.

"Jesus, you're a fast learner!" I scream, and he covers my mouth again.

"Do you squirt like I do?" he asks, genuinely curious.

I can only nod, my moans turning into whimpers as his thumb expertly learns to go in circles rather than flick. He slows the circles down, increasing the pressure.

"Cover your own mouth, Xanthe... I want to watch you squirt..."

He releases my mouth and I cover it myself with both hands. He tilts his hips back and his cock finds my g-spot like a heat seeking missile. He watches as he fucks me, careful and sure with his thumb on my clit, and god do I squirt.

I didn't think I would actually do it, so it shocks me as much as it shocks him. I arch my back, desperately holding my hands over my mouth as I writhe and scream. Brec slows his thrusts but hits my cervix with more power, more intent, the grin on his face full of pride. As I reach my climax a second time, his eyes grow wide with astonishment and he can no longer focus. He collapses over me, crushing me with his body as he spasms with his final release.

I clutch him, completely drunk on sex, and kiss him every-where. I kiss his shoulder, his neck, his chin, and when his mouth finds mine, I taste myself on his lips and almost lose my mind.

"Brec…" I whisper into his ear and he shivers as I say his name. "Want to learn something else?" His head shoots up and he nods excitedly. The change from brooding vampire to pleasing puppy is the sexiest thing I've ever seen. "I want you to kiss me—" I start, but his mouth crashes to mine eagerly and I shake my head, gently pushing him away. "I want you to kiss me… here…" I slide my hand between us and he kisses down, following my hand until he's on his knees looking at the core of me.

"Here?" he asks. If the man had a tail, it would be wagging. I nod, and he kisses gently, just a kiss. I growl quietly and put my hand on his head and push his face against my clit.

"Unless it's too much…" I add the last part as a dare and he growls deep in his throat at the challenge.

His tongue darts out and he licks me from my rear entrance to the top of my clit. I arch my back and barely remember to cover my mouth before I'm screaming again. Just like when he was fucking me, he watches for what I like the most and repeats it. His tongue dips inside me, and he looks up at me with his own cum on his face.

"Like this, kitten?" he growls, prideful as I squirm.

"Suck… lightly… here…" I spread my labia and rub the tip of my clit with my middle finger.

"You better cover your mouth again," he growls as he sucks my clit into his mouth and the vibration of the growl and the pressure of the sucking make me come right away.

I'm screaming so loud now that people walking by are commenting 'the doctor is in' before they laugh and run away. Brec is back to licking gently as the throes of pleasure slowly ebb away, and when he's cleaned every trace of him from me, he stands and wipes his mouth with the back of his hand.

I have to smile as I look up at him, he's so proud. Hell, I'm proud. He went from virgin to best sex I've ever had in one session. I can't wait to show him all the different positions. He leans over me, rubbing his half-hard cock against me as he pulls me to his chest and we lay together on the desk.

"Xanthe? Do you have an answer for me? Will you be my pretend soulmate?"

He grins at me, and I could watch him grin like that for the rest of my life. I wrap my arms around his neck and lick his nose.

"What the hell, you only live once, right? Keep fucking me like this and I might give you the whole month."

He kisses me, and the kiss is somehow different. Tender, thankful, exhausted. I don't know how much longer I have to live, but what a way to spend my last days. Fuck it, I'll live this week to the fullest and fuck this amazing monster every chance I get. When he's done with me, I'll go somewhere and die on my own terms.

They say drowning is peaceful, maybe an ocean cruise then. No one will have to worry about what to do with my body.

"How do you know this doctor's schedule?" he asks, nuzzling my neck.

"I spend my weekends here looking after Mara."

And I used to work with him. I omit that part, he took over the specialty when I stepped down. This used to be my office.

Brec lays his head on my chest and his brows knit together as he listens to my heart. His head shoots up, confused, and he goes to ask a question but I kiss him again.

"I need to tell Doug I'll be out for the week. We should get dressed."

"Why tell him anything? I own this whole building. If I say you're working for me for a week, then he can't say anything different." He hugs me close, possessively, and kisses me again.

I laugh and push him off, standing up and twisting out of his reach before he can catch me. He glowers, shadows appearing around him as he stands and stalks closer. I feel a spark of terror as his eyes glint in the dim light.

"Doug is my friend, if I just disappear he'll get worried..."

"Doug has a claim on you?" he snarls, baring his teeth and backing me in a corner.

"N..no... he doesn't, it's just the polite thing to do, you know?"

Brec pins me to the wall, and the shadows around him block out the entire office. All I can see is him, and his glorious cock standing ready again. I reach for him, trying to stop my hands from trembling as I touch his chest. "I'm yours, Brec." I smile gently, and quickly correct myself. "For the week." I clear my throat and duck out from under his arms but he grabs me around the hips and pulls my back to him.

He nuzzles my neck, his fangs scratching lightly on my shoulder. "For the month..." He demands, his cock twitching between my butt cheeks.

"Brec, we had a deal..." I moan as he strokes the back of his hand down my side and inside my legs.

"I want you again..." he whispers, his voice gruff. "Do people fuck like this? Could I just bend you over and fuck you like this?"

I shiver with pleasure but twist out of his grasp.

"I'm tired, I'm hungry, and I desperately need a shower. Let me go say goodbye and then you can take me home... and I'll show you all the different ways people can fuck," I tell him as I dress myself, and with a wink I slip out of the office.

As I walk away, I can see his shadows seeping out from under the door. There's a part of me, deep in my core, that is carnally afraid of Brec, but battling that is my horny little cunt, and I can't wait to have him inside me again.

"Jesus, Xanthe! Are you alright?" Doug rushes towards me, seeing my flushed face and messy hair. He grabs his walkie talkie. "Do I need to call someone in here? Are you having another spell?"

"What spells?" I turn around to see Brec looming over me, his gray eyes looking at Doug as if he'd rip him to shreds if he dared to lay a hand on me.

Doug takes two quick steps back and holds his hands up defensively as Brec's hand slips around my waist possessively and steps in front of me.

"Doug, you know Mr. Cadell right? Our boss?" I try to look at Doug from behind Brec but he's leaning over Doug as if he poses some threat. I'm incredibly proud when Doug squares his shoulders and points his finger directly at Brec.

"I don't know what you want with her but I swear to god if it's malicious I don't care who you are!"

Brec's lips peel back from his teeth and the room gets darker, but I dart between them and push Doug away.

"Are you crazy? He signs your paychecks, you idiot!" I whisper fiercely.

"You need me to do something? Is he threatening you? I don't care what happens to me, I'll protect you!"

I smile, poor Doug is so fierce and protective like a father. I hug him quickly and Brec snarls.

"Everything is ok, he needs me for a private security gig. High steaks. Undercover. He's just stressed, but there's nothing to worry about."

"You're sure?" Doug looks deep into my eyes and I take both

his hands in mine, making Brec bristle. I kinda enjoy the jealousy, but I nod to Doug and turn to Brec, happily smiling and moving back to his side.

"No matter what she says..." Doug starts, and I cringe. He has no idea who he's fucking with here. "The people she works with, including myself, are her family. Only ones she's got. You hurt her and I'll come for you, I don't give a rat's ass who you are."

"Xanthe will be safe with me, no harm will come to her while she's in my care." Brec glares at Doug as he pulls me under his arm. His muscles are tense, twitching, he's ready to strike.

I snake an arm around his back and start pushing him out the door. I'm touched that he thinks he can protect me, but no one can save me from fate.

"See ya, Doug! Text me if anything juicy happens!" I close the door and Brec looks down at me.

"He has your phone number? Why? I don't even have that." He glares between me and the door.

"Jesus, would you relax? He has my number because he's my partner, er... my work partner." I correct myself when Brec tries to move back towards the door. "Take me home, Brec. I think a bubble bath sounds like just the right thing..."

I pull on his shirt as I talk about taking a bath and his predatory eyes focus back on me entirely. When he bares his teeth this time, I know it's for a completely different emotion. He turns on a heel, my hand in his, and drags me to the roof and into his helicopter. Brec isn't gonna fuck around, he puts me on his lap as soon as he's seated and slips his hands in my pants.

As the helicopter takes off I start moaning, how a virgin can become so advanced so quickly is beyond me. Thankfully the helicopter is loud enough that even I can't hear myself scream in pleasure.

CHAPTER 6

BREC

As the helicopter lands on the rooftop of my penthouse, I slip my fingers out of Xanthe and into her mouth. She sucks my fingers like she sucked my cock, and I turn to shadow and carry her out of the helicopter before we've even fully landed. I finally set her down in the foyer of my penthouse and she looks around with wide eyes.

Centuries of history adorn the walls, my first suit of armor, my last roman headdress. All the weapons I've ever wielded line the walls. I lead her into the main living area that has only marble stools and glass display cases filled with items from my past.

"This is impressive...for a museum." She smiles at me. "Don't you ever need to be comfortable? Where's the couch, the TV? Do you never relax here?"

I look at her, confused. "I have a comfortable chair in my office."

Xanthe rolls her eyes. "You're gonna have to let me add some feminine touches if you want anyone to believe this is real." She smirks at me and I start pulling her clothes off, shredding them. "You're a machine!" She shoves me back and laughs.

"What? I want you, now." I growl deep in my throat, shredding my own clothes and stalking towards her like a lion. "I want to fuck you over this bench, I want to lick you on the mantle, I want to take you from behind in the kitchen and on the floor and—"

"Brec! Focus!" She puts both hands on either side of my face and shakes me a little bit. "You may not need to rest, but I'm only human!"

I do my best to calm myself, taking deep breaths and exhaling growls. I don't know what it is about her, but I have an animalistic need to breed her. To taste her blood, now. I try to grab her and she twists out of my grasp.

"If you ever want to see this again—" she cups the mound between her legs and backs away. "You'll order me some tacos and tequila and show me where the bathroom is or I'll get myself off without you all. Night. Long."

With a groan of frustration, I point to a pair of French doors across the room and pull my cell phone out. As she walks away she looks over her shoulder, flaunting the power she has over me.

I'll order her food, that's for sure, and then remind her in that bath that I don't actually need to breathe. My cock stands at attention as I order catering for a party from my assistant. I tell him to bring it into the display room and to not disturb me, no matter what he hears. While I confirm it all I hear the bath start to run, then Xanthe humming in the bathroom. If she thinks she's going to clean herself without me, she's sorely mistaken. I hang up the phone while my assistant is explaining everything is closed. I know he'll find a way.

I open the French doors just as she's sinking that tight tan body into the huge bathtub overflowing with bubbles. I stroke my cock as I watch her wet her hair. "There are things we're going to have to discuss," I say as I walk towards her.

She watches me like a siren in the water.

"Battle tactics?" she asks, laying down in the water.

Precum drips from me as I watch her dark nipples break the surface.

"Rules, how you should behave around..." I choke on my words as she moans. "Are you touching yourself?" I demand, and she nods, moaning again.

"Did you order my food?" she asks, her voice teasing.

"It will arrive within the hour." I step into the bath and rip her hand off her mound. "That's *my* job," I hiss at her and sink under the water.

She gasps as my mouth sucks her clit automatically, and for a moment she starts to panic and worry about me, but I pin her hips to my mouth and fuck her with my tongue.

I surface long enough to speak. "That's right...vampire... no...breathing..."

She says no more after that, just writhes in pleasure.

I let my thumb linger on her rear entrance and she gasps, and when I put my thumb inside she comes instantly. I grin against her squirting pussy...fucking good to know. I don't let her rest, don't let her catch her breath, I put my thumb all the way in, exploring her hot passage with my tongue and rubbing my nose against her clit.

I'm full of pride, so much that I feel my chest could burst, as she comes again and again. Finally she begs me to stop, and I rise out of the water and lean against the other side of the enormous tub to watch her catch her breath. She looks paler than usual, her breathing more labored than before. I sit up with a start when I see her hand on her chest and she chuckles.

"Down boy, I'm just...really tired."

Something about what she says doesn't seem completely truthful. I scoot towards her, slipping her body over mine and letting her rest on my chest. She thinks I'm being sweet. She even sighs quietly and cuddles close, but I'm trying to hear her heart again. I put my hands on her breast, kissing her neck and counting her heartbeats and her breaths. There's something not right about the sound of her heart, but I can't put my finger on it.

Xanthe scoots slightly and my cock slides inside her. I gasp in surprise, my mind going completely blank. "I told you fucking like this is possible..."

She moans, her heartbeat picking up its uneven rhythm as she rocks herself on my cock. It doesn't take long with her riding me so gently that I push worries about her heart from my mind. Maybe all humans sound like that these days anyway, how would I know? She's the only human I've paid attention to in centuries.

I can sense she's tiring, so I gently lift her to her knees and kneel behind her. "Humans fuck so many ways..." I chuckle as I slowly slip myself back to where I belong, balls deep inside her.

Her moaning starts to grow wild and I go from sensually pulling in and out of her to pounding her until her shrieks start to become desperate whimpers as she reaches her climax. A warm rush escapes her body under the water, scorching my cock as she starts to quake and shiver as she comes. My own body coils, drawing in, contracting to the one point we meet as I thrust and thrust, my own release hanging on a precipice—

The door to the bathroom bursts open.

"My brother! I knew it wouldn't be long!" Adam declares, marching into the bathroom with his hands on his hips. "Oh, I see you're getting the job started, now what you need to do is lean over and bite her right here." Adam touches her neck with one finger and I fly out of the tub, pinning him against the wall and roaring.

I'm not sure what comes over me, but seeing my brother

touch her made me want to rip him limb from limb. Adam roars back at me, both our fangs bared, when Kiera walks in.

"Are you kidding me, Adam? I told you to wait!"

Shocked, I stop and stare at Kiera. Her stomach is huge, protruding out like a basketball, but as she walks toward my petrified Xanthe and helps her out of the bath, she doesn't look pregnant at all from the back. "You two get out of here. You've scared this girl so bad her heart is skipping beats! Out!"

Adam and I walk out of the room like chastised children, and Kiera throws a towel at my face. I take it quickly, wiping the suds off my body and glaring at Adam. "What right do you have to break into my home and interrupt mating like this?" I demand, and Adam looks at me and laughs. All anger from the altercation in the bathroom forgotten.

"I didn't break in, Mateo heard about your food order when your assistant called to get his help. He figured with Mateo's heritage he'd know where to get taco." Adam laughs again and walks over to a full table of tacos and salt and limes and several bottles of tequila. "I knew the only reason you'd be ordering anything but blood is if you had a human to feed." Adam winks at me and sits on one of the benches. "You sure found a pretty thing! I'm excited to have a sister in our family."

I growl at my brother and pace the floor in front of him. I haven't prepared Xanthe for this, she only knows she has to pretend. I'd planned on explaining everything over dinner; what I expect from her, how she should act, how to be convincing enough to pass as my Forever Bound without me ever having to prove I won't be changing her.

Kiera and Xanthe walk out of the bathroom smiling ear to ear, Xanthe wearing the Egyptian cotton robe I bought for myself and never used. It fits her so loosely that I can see her breasts when she turns to the side. I turned to shadow, coming between her and Kiera and closing the robe better. I pull Xanthe away from them, trying to hide her, trying to keep them from seeing her. Something about them being here makes me fiercely protective and I want to take her away from here and never look back.

Xanthe's warm hands find my face in the darkness of my shadow and she kisses me. "It's alright," she whispers. "I like her. Your brother though...needs to learn some boundaries." She laughs as Kiera slaps Adam in the back of the head and starts scolding him about listening to his mate when he's told to wait for people to finish their sexcapades.

"How far along are you, Kiera?" Xanthe asks as she removes herself from my protection.

I have to take several steadying breaths before I can regain my normal form and banish the shadows. I turn to face my family and my woman just as Xanthe places her hands on Kiera's belly. I would never in my life harm a woman, but seeing Xanthe touch anyone me makes me insane. Bristling, I sit on a bench opposite Adam and listen to the women talk.

"About three months." Kiera smiles as Xanthe's eyes widen. "Forever Bound babies aren't your typical pregnancy. Are you a doctor? That would be so convenient right about now!"

"Oh, no no, I just know a few things about babies. May I?" Xanthe motions lifting Kiera's shirt and she obliges, and Adam sits straighter and narrows his eyes.

I immediately jump to my feet and grab Adam by the collar and drag him out of my penthouse and to the roof in a flash of shadow. The women's laughter echoes behind us.

"I don't want to fight you, Adam, but if you look at Xanthe like you're going to hurt her one more time, I will." I bare my teeth at him and Adam runs a hand through his long hair and has the decency to look abashed.

"It's not her, I swear," he starts. "It's the baby, whenever someone gets near Kiera's belly, I can't control myself. I want her to go to the villa in the alps with me for the rest of the pregnancy but she refuses. Too many bad memories. I don't want to tell her how many more bad memories she'll have if someone touches my child without my consent..." I lunge at him, my talons ready to rip him to shreds. "Jesus, Brec, I didn't mean I'd do it to Xanthe! I'm just thinking out loud! Calm the hell down!"

I freeze, my claws a mere fraction from his neck. What is wrong with me? She's not even my real mate. The protectiveness helps my case, but I know I need to calm down. "Just... just stay away from her. Don't look at her, even, not until I can change her. Not until things calm down..." I demand in a fierce whisper, walking away from him and bracing my hands on the railings around the roof's landing pad, staring out at the expanse of Sorin City beneath us.

"Speaking of which, don't fight it. Do it tonight, get it done and make her stronger. We need all the people we can get in fighting condition. Kiera's mother is ordering the mobilization of her forces; it seems she's taken control of the Monroe clan. Or maybe she already was? Now that we know she exists, there's no use hiding their hierarchy." Adam joins me and leans on the railing. "It makes sense that a female leads them; Kiera is insanely strong, with the ability to glamor other vampires. The other day, she had me convinced there was a rat in the kitchen. I searched for hours before returning to our chambers to find she'd lied so she could set up the baby's cot next to our bed. She wanted to surprise me."

I try to force myself to relax, this is my brother not my competition. He already has a mate and he dotes over her. Xanthe isn't even mine and yet I'm acting like Adam does with Kiera. Frustrated, I rub the back of my neck and start to apologize for acting so rashly when I hear Keira call from the window of the penthouse.

"Excuse me? Bickering boys? I'm tired and I want to go home now!"

Adam rolls his eyes and steps away. "She was so excited to come here and meet your woman, and now she's ready to go. Pregnancy is no joke, she could fall asleep standing up!"

Adam and Kiera are already in the foyer, ready to leave, and this time Adam makes sure to stay far away from Xanthe with a knowing glance. Scowling, I place a possessive arm around Xanthe's waist, telling myself it's for the pretense that she's my Forever Bound.

Xanthe and Kiera make a date for a proper pregnancy exam with our private doctors. Turns out Xanthe's very interested in the transition from human to vampire and the changes that a body goes through, and how one could carry a child after. There's a distant sadness in her eyes as they leave and her hand lingers on her own stomach. When she turns to look at me, she tries to smile but it doesn't reach her eyes.

"Are you alright? I know that was...a lot." I glare at my brother as he leaves and take Xanthe's arm, leading her to the kitchen where she quickly grabs a taco and a bottle of tequila and sits on the edge of the table.

I take a deep annoyed breath and pull a chair out for her, indicating the proper way to eat at a table. She only grins as she sits, the minx knows exactly what she's doing.

I try a different tactic. "I know we didn't have a chance to talk before your first meeting with members of my family, but I have rules you need to know about. There's a way you must act for this to work, and you must never *ever* go near another man in my presence again."

Xanthe raises an eyebrow as she takes a bite of her taco. I can see her resisting the urge to roll her eyes and I grind my teeth.

"As a Forever Bound you will be akin to a queen, and you

have to act like one. That means sitting up straight, eating with a plate, and using a napkin when making a mess..." I narrow my eyes at her as she drops lettuce on my table when taking a bite. This time she does roll her eyes but reaches for a napkin and cleans up her mess.

"So many rules for a week of sex..." She smirks, trying to get a rise out of me.

I ignore her. "When we go to the castle—" I start to say and Xanthe spits food all over the table.

"Castle? There's a castle?" She's shocked, but she quickly tries to clean up her mess once more. She sits on the table again and I bristle. "I've never even seen a castle, is there one here in Sorin City somewhere? What, is it underground?" She chuckles and takes a swig of tequila and puts her bare foot up on the chair she's supposed to be sitting in, exposing her thigh.

All thoughts of irritation leave my mind as I glimpse the curls between her thighs. If I do drink from her, I want the first bite to be right there, next to the hot sweetness of her core.

Xanthe notices the shift in my demeanor and rubs her thigh slowly, drawing lines up and down as she talks. "I'll behave however you want in the presence of your family, Brec, but when we're alone I'm going to be myself. You picked me for this farce because of who I am, not because of what you thought I could pretend to be. Don't try and say that's not true. You like me, you can't deny that. You just wanted an excuse to have me all to yourself."

She gets fully on the table and crawls over to me, wrapping her arms around my neck.

"You wanted me, and now you have me. You can keep being the miserable vampire jaded by his family duty or you can lick tequila off my chest." She lifts the bottle and pours it slowly into her cleavage.

I'm almost jealous of the way the liquor gets to run over her skin. Obediently, I lick it up as I slowly open her robe and bare her beautiful body for only me to see.

"You are being naughty, kitten..." I murmur as I flick one of her nipples with my tongue.

"You didn't get to finish in the tub, and I never got to get clean. So how about we get this table absolutely filthy?" Xanthe reaches down between us and rips the towel off my waist and smiles as she sees I'm already hard and ready. "Want to learn another position that humans like to do?"

All I can do is nod.

Breathless, I watch her lay on her back on the table. She hangs her head off the edge and pulls my throbbing cock into her mouth. She sucks me so hard and so deep into her mouth that I lose my balance and have to brace myself on the table.

I watch, enraptured, as she rubs tequila over her body for me to lick off. She rubs it lower, lower, until I'm licking tequila from her clit.

I have a lot to learn this week, and maybe just maybe, there won't be time for her to visit the castle at all.

CHAPTER 7

XANTHE

I wake up the next morning tangled in the sheets and alone. Brec's bedroom is nothing but a mattress on the floor and not even a comfortable one. I guess for a man who doesn't need to sleep things like that don't matter, but if I'm going to be sleeping here for the next week, I better get a proper bed, even if it's just the one from my place.

I sit up and stretch, missing my bed for more reasons than one as I realize how stiff I am and how difficult it's going to be to stand up off the floor. I struggle to my feet after detangling myself from the sheets and cringe as my joints pop and crackle. I'm not old enough to be creaking like an old door hinge!

With a glance over my shoulder, I grab my purse and quickly take the cocktail of drugs that keep the pain of my failing body at bay. Shoving the vials deep into the recesses, I tuck my purse back against the mattress, a tinge of guilt making me wince. Brec's been sweet enough to make sure my belongings were here when I woke, and trusting enough not to go through them.

He's going to make some woman very happy someday.

I tiptoe to the connected bathroom, trying not to alert Brec that I'm awake. I need a long hot soak in the shower, and I'd prefer it to be alone. I need to think about everything that's happening and how I'm going to disconnect from Brec when the week is over. There's no way I'll be able to continue working for him, not after all this, and I can't let him into my life permanently. It's just not an option. I turn on the shower and test the water with my hand and to my surprise, I find I'm sad to have to push him away like I've pushed everyone else.

Still, no one needs to see what's coming.

As I step into the hot shower, I shiver with pleasure. The water's just hot enough to turn my olive skin bright red, just shy of scalding. It feels absolutely amazing. As I rinse myself, I look around the shower at all the doodads and levers it has. Since when is a shower not just a shower? I press a button that has several water drops drawn on it and the whole ceiling starts raining. Delighted, I step into the center of the deluge and turn in place, relishing the hot rain. Okay, so this is way better than a normal shower!

I start looking at the buttons in more detail, this one has a musical note on it. I push it and screaming rock music blasts louder than I ever imagined. I'm so startled I slip, falling and landing on my ass right as Brec bursts through the door. I can't hear him over the song; 'nymphetamine nymphetamine nymphetamine girl.' What in the world is a nymphetamine girl and why are they screaming it? Brec helps me to my feet as a woman's voice joins the screaming and I have to admit that part of the song is actually nice. He reaches over and shuts the music off.

"Are you alright? I'll program that later to be something you like." He helps me up and I rest in his arms, getting his naked body all wet. He steps in the shower with me and pulls me close. "I was just about to join you when I heard the music and I saw you fall." He kisses the top of my head and massages my ass with both hands. "Only thing pounding on this should be me..." He chuckles, but the chuckle turns into a growl as his cock gets hard against my stomach.

I can't help it, there's something about him that calms and comforts me. I wanted this shower to be solo but as he holds me, I can't help but to melt against his strong chest. I breathe in the musky scent of him as he pours shampoo on my hair and starts massaging my scalp. I could purr, it feels that good.

"Interesting choice of music," I murmur as he turns me around to work the soap down to the ends of my hair. "It really fits your 'I'm a big scary vampire' vibe."

He chuckles and rinses my hair with the actual shower spout. "To each their own, right? What did you expect?"

"I dunno, classical? Maybe some Bach or Beethoven? You're a vampire, centuries old. Never expected screamo." I try to turn to face him, but he forces me back.

"I'm not done, the conditioner is next." His hands are like vices, but so tender and warm on my skin that I don't bother to fight him.

"I know how to wash my own hair, Brec." I look over my shoulder at him and the 'don't mess with me' glare on his face has me shutting up quick.

"This is a pleasure for me, your hair is like a cloud. I want to catch it and tame it, but also let it wave wild and free." He rinses my hair again but then grabs a washer and makes it nice and sudsy. He pulls me against his chest and begins washing my breasts. "This is a pleasure for me in other ways..." He nibbles my ear as his hands venture further down to wash me between my legs. "I've made such a mess of you all night, it's only right that I clean up."

"You're making me want to start another mess..." I gasp as he turns me to face him and washes my back and my ass.

"Don't you worry, we have all day to get messy again. I've

cleared my entire schedule just to see how long you can sit on my face before you can't handle it anymore." His face is so serious, but as soon as the soap is rinsed completely away, he pulls up my leg and sinks deep inside my core. "You wouldn't think I'd miss this after just a few hours," he gasps and I moan, attempting to climb him and ride him in the shower. His cock is so thick and amazing, I can't help myself.

"I actually have stuff I have to do today, so let's make this fast and wonderful."

He stops mid stroke and pulls out, scowling. "You told me I get a week, that means you are *mine*. You're not going anywhere."

I get out and wrap myself in a towel and scowl at him while he bristles back at me. "No, I said I would pretend to be your Forever Bound for a week. I never said I'd stop my life and my plans." I stand there, chin held high and hands on my hips and dare him to challenge me.

Brec turns off the shower and stalks out in all his naked vampire glory. "What do you even have to do that's better than this?" He pulls me against his body and wraps my hand around his cock.

"You give a new definition to the term cocky, Brec Cadell!" As much as my body reacts to his naked nearness, I snatch my hand away from him and storm out of the bathroom to get dressed in my uniform since he never gave me a chance to collect an overnight bag. I have responsibilities. "If you must know, *my lord*, I volunteer at a soup kitchen every Sunday afternoon and stop in to see Mara in the evening. I'm going to go and there's nothing you can do to stop me." I watch him from the corner of my eye, waiting to see how he'll react to being told no. I have the sense that no one's ever tried before.

Brec clenches and unclenches his fists, his jaw working as he glares at me. I glare back, hoping to hell he doesn't get back in my personal space. I've already learned self-control isn't a term that exists around this man. And for some reason, this is important. I don't have much in my life since I received the ill-fated news, but what I do, I treasure.

Finally, he heaves a heavy sigh and goes over to his closet and starts getting dressed. He tosses me a bag from a local boutique. "I went out and got you some clothes this morning, and since I'm accompanying you, I would hope you could wear something you don't work in every day."

"You're coming?" I'm shocked as I catch the bag in midair, discovering it's my favorite boutique. Inside is a white cotton blouse and a jean jacket with a pair of dark wash jeans and patent leather boots. Everything is the right size. "How did you know my size?"

"Of course I'm coming, I said you're mine for the week and that means where you go I go." He raises a brow at me and points at my uniform and discarded converse. "I checked your size first, and you had a receipt from the boutique in your jacket pocket."

I have to stop and think, plopping myself down on the bed to get dressed. Is this endearing? Creepy? Both? We're just acting, right? Even as I think that my heart strings tug a little bit. I need this week to go by fast, I cannot be falling for a vampire; even if there weren't any outstanding circumstances, it will never work.

"Well, you better be on your best behavior. No better than thou airs and no scaring the piss out of the homeless. You have rules and so do I. If you're coming with me, you're helping out. End of discussion." I get up from the bed much easier now that my muscles have relaxed in the shower and I sashay by him with a huff.

He grabs my arm, pulling me back and tilting my chin up to his mouth where he steals a kiss. "The first chance I get, we're finishing what we started in the shower," he growls, and I get hot and bothered instantly.

Gone is our little disagreement as his cock gets hard in his jeans. If I wasn't already running late, I'd pull down the pants he bought me and let him take me right here against the wall. He seems to see the fire in my eyes and for a second it feels like he can read my mind, but a voice comes over the speakers through the house to announce the car has been readied for us.

"How did anyone know we were leaving?" I say, shocked.

"They didn't, I bought you a car. I also found your bus ticket in your pocket."

"You have got to be kidding me! I said I don't want your money!" I stomp my foot and he smirks at me, walking out the door without another word. Fuming, I follow, and he leads me down thirty stories in the elevator and into a private basement garage. There, in all its glory, is a bright yellow Jeep Wrangler with black trim. I can't help it, I shriek in excitement.

"There's no way you could have known this was my dream car, Brec!" I beam at him as I run up to the jeep and an attendant jumps out and tosses me the keys.

"I may or may not have had a discussion with Doug. He's very concerned about you taking public transportation." He reaches over me and buckles me into the driver's seat. "Why would he be so worried?"

I go stiff as he asks the question. "A woman alone in the big city? Anything can happen, you know." I bite my lip as he raises a brow at me, his hand lingering on my thigh as he leans in for a kiss.

I sink into it, mostly because I haven't tasted him in a good twenty minutes, but also because I don't want him thinking too hard about that question.

"Thank you, by the way..." I breathe as he breaks the kiss and steps away, closing the door behind him.

Grinning, I quickly start the car and act like I'm going to peel out, but he slams both hands on the hood of the jeep and glares at me while shaking his head. If I had any sense at all that glare would terrify me, but I can't wait to see what that glare looks like when I'm sitting in his face.

The soup kitchen is packed, homeless people rounding corners for blocks in line. I glance at Brec as we walk through the doors, waiting to see if he cringes at the smell or glares at anyone. He just watches me, watches where I go, who gets too close, checking all the exits and taking note of every security camera.

"This building is not secure," he grumbles as I put on an apron and toss him one.

The food has already been made, chili and cornbread, good for a cooler day like today. As we're serving it, the homeless population refuses to make eye contact with Brec. He's been designated to handing out napkins.

"Miss Xanthe, who's this tall drink of water?" Gail, my dearest street friend asks me. She's wearing trash bags over her tattered clothes and they're dripping with water. I hadn't realized it was raining.

"Good afternoon, Miss Gail, this here? He's my bodyguard!" I whisper the last bit to her behind my gloved hand and she giggles. "Are you staying warm enough, Gail, is there anything I can do to help?"

Gail takes her food and then takes a napkin from Brec as she winks and blows him a kiss. "I could use one of these!" she jokes, pointing at Brec as she walks away laughing.

Brec's first glare of the night is mine and mine alone.

"I am not your bodyguard," he declares, and when he's sure no one's looking he squeezes my ass. "I'm your lover, get it right."

The possessive glint in his eyes makes my knees grow weak and I glance at my watch, almost wishing it was time to go home already.

When we arrive at the hospital hours later, I can't sit still, I'm so aroused and needy that it makes it hard to drive. Brec's cock is hard, but he makes a point to act like he's ignoring me as he watches the buildings on the way to the hospital go by. That act in itself, him being hard but respectful enough not to distract me while driving, makes me want to pull over. Just then, my phone rings and I press the bluetooth button so I can hear it over the car speakers.

"Xan, it's Doug. Mara's coding."

My heart drops almost as fast as my foot on the pedal. I go from a leisurely drive to racing down the highway, cutting cars off and risking both our lives.

"How long?" I demand. "What's her condition?"

"It's not good. She looks like she stopped breathing," Doug says in hushed tones.

The moment I stop in front of the hospital, the car goes black with shadow. I feel Brec pick me up, and faster than lightning, we're in the children's ward. I give him a thankful smile and run from him and straight to Mara. The room is full of nurses, but no doctors.

"Where's her attending?" I demand.

"He's coming as fast as he can, are you the mother?" one nurse says as she squeezes a bag to get air into Mara.

"Move aside," I demand, taking the bag and checking Mara's pulse. In quick succession I order medication and treatment, telling each nurse where to go and what to do and who to call. "Why aren't you moving? We're losing her! Go! STAT!"

The nurses jump into motion, shocked as I've completely taken over the scene.

"Brec, take over compressions. You know how, right?"

Brec walks over immediately, though he looks shocked as well. He starts compressions with just the right amount of pressure and I thank my lucky stars. Soon the nurses are back, and one hands me a large needle and tube.

"Her lung has collapsed," I say to no one in particular as I open Mara's gown and find the right place between her ribs. Brec backs away as I puncture the tiny little girl's skin, carefully inserting the tube, my lips moving in a silent prayer.

I feel the moment it penetrates her lung, followed by a flow of pink liquid, and Mara finally takes her first breath on her own.

My knees go weak. "Mara? Baby, can you hear me?" I stroke her forehead as her eyes flutter open.

"My angel..." she whispers, and falls unconscious again just as her doctor walks in the room.

He gives me a knowing look and only nods as I grab Brec's hand and lead him out of the room.

CHAPTER 8

BREC

As I lead Xanthe down the stairs to her car, I can feel her tremble. It's clear how she feels about the little girl, but now that she's stable, her doctor informed us the sedatives will ensure Mara won't be conscious until morning.

All thoughts of playful banter and sex are pushed to the back of my mind, for all I can think about is if Xanthe's alright. When we get to her car, I take her to the passenger side and help her in. She frowns, but doesn't fight me. The drive home is a silent one, in which Xanthe wipes away soundless tears.

We walk quietly to the elevator and inside I just hold her as she weeps. I'm already wondering what I can do to help—food? A warm bath again? Humans seem to like wine at times like this...—when a strange scraping sound reaches my ears. Then what sounds like footsteps. Voices.

The closer we get to the penthouse, the louder it gets and the more alert I become. Xanthe's experienced enough pain today. If there's anyone here with the intent to hurt her, they won't live to see another second.

The doors open on dozens of men moving furniture and

Kiera in the middle of them all, holding her belly up as she struggles to walk around.

She spins around at their entrance, her face going from frustrated to annoyed. "Brec! You're home too soon! Leave again!" she demands, but then she sees Xanthe, tear stained and wiped out. "Everyone out!" she orders, and all the people drop what they're doing and go to the balcony outside to await further instructions. Kiera waddles to Xanthe and takes her in her arms with a fierce glare at me. "What did you do, you big oaf!" she hisses at me as she pets Xanthe's hair. Xan has completely melted down now, sobbing loudly against Kiera, just as the elevator dings again and Adam and Mateo walk in.

"Handle your brother, Adam, before I do," Kiera barks, and the look she gives me feels as if she's throwing daggers into my chest. She guides Xanthe out of the room with a fierce glance for all three of us men.

"What did you do?" Adam asks, shocked, as Mateo starts laughing.

"If I know Brec at all, whatever he did he doesn't know he did it!" Mateo says over his shoulder as he pushes a cart of brand new women's clothes past us and into my bedroom... where there's now a four-post bed draped with white curtains and other various furniture scattered around.

"I didn't do anything, Adam," I tell my brother, and his face softens. "There's a little girl she cares about, she's very sick. She almost died tonight."

Adam puts his hand on my shoulder and squeezes. "Human emotions can be absolutely wild before they change. Once she's one of us, she'll be much better at processing things and less weepy."

"I don't want her to be anything less..." I say as I look at the hallway they disappeared down. "What is going on here, anyway?" I turn to my brother and his eyebrows shoot up in the most 'it wasn't me' expression I've ever seen.

"I don't stand in Kiera's way, brother. She said your home wasn't livable, and she decided to fix it." He walks away from me without another word, slipping into the kitchen like he's running away.

"When Xanthe is changed, she won't walk all over me like Kiera does to you!" I shout behind him.

"Wanna bet?" Keira says from behind me and I brace myself for a blow to the head, but all that comes is Xanthe's arms slipping around my waist. I wrap my arms around her and look over her head at Kiera, who glares a warning and walks by me to join Adam in the kitchen.

"I'm sorry," Xanthe whispers.

"You have nothing to be sorry about, kitten," I say as she tilts her head up to me. She's now wearing comfortable lounging pajamas and bunny slippers.

"Kiera did all this for us, isn't it amazing?" She waves around the house and pretends as if I don't know she's just changed the subject.

Mateo walks out of the kitchen and nods to me. "Marianna has dinner ready on the table. Are you guys hungry?"

Adam and I dutifully nod, even though human food offers us no sustenance. We eat is purely to fit it.

We follow him into the kitchen to see an entire Sunday dinner spread over my huge kitchen table. My connecting living room is in disarray, most of my collection has been moved to the wall and white couches set up in a cozy manner next to an electric fireplace and a huge, big-screen TV.

Xanthe squeals with delight as Mateo pulls a chair out for her and Marianna serves her a plate of ham and potatoes and green beans. Behind her, in the kitchen proper, Rodger is slipping a cake in the oven and smiling from ear to ear at his wife.

As we all sit down to dinner, I find I'm speechless. A warm feeling has taken over my chest, almost making me...relaxed. Seeing my brother and his wife, and even our human companions, around the table brings me alive in a way I've never felt. I take Xanthe's hand and smile at her as she tells an animated story about taking down gangsters in the ER. I make an internal note to hire additional security for outside the building.

"Is that an actual smile?" Adam asks just as Mateo snaps a picture.

"Photo or it didn't happen!" he smirks, and I go quickly back to frowning.

Xanthe smiles at me and squeezes my hand.

"Xan, you're good for him. I was beginning to think he was born without the muscles to smile at all!" Adam grins from ear to ear and I imagine throwing a slice of ham at his face. "Which reminds me, when is the big day? The cease fire won't hold long. You better get down to business."

I slam my hand on the table and the wood splinters. Everyone jumps and Xanthe looks afraid. "Cease fire?" she whispers, but I get up from the table and drag my brother to the balcony with me. The men here have long since gone back to setting up, discreetly and quietly. If I didn't know they were here, I'd think it was just us.

"Don't bring that up in front of Xanthe again," I hiss at my brother and he rolls his eyes, leaning on arm on the banister.

"Putting it off helps no one, drain her and get it over with. She's your mate, brother, a blind man could see that!"

"I will not risk her life until I'm certain! I will not do what our father did! I refuse." I clench my fists on the banister and look away from Adam, who sighs.

"It will be fine, she will wake up and everything will be as it was meant to be.

"And if she doesn't? If she dies?" I demand, and my chest

grows heavy at the thought. Xanthe dead, gone, because of me. I almost vomit.

"She won't die, Brec. She's strong. Her heart goes crazy when she sees you, I'm sure you've heard it. I've found my Forever Bound, so I know what it looks like. She's the one, brother."

I glare at him and scowl, but I nod. I cannot deny that the longer I spend with Xanthe the more I feel like she could actually be the one after all. I won't ever change her, I don't need to find out. I can love her as she is for the rest of my days and never risk her life.

Adam takes my nod as consent and goes back to the dining room and collects everyone to leave.

"Brec and Xan have a long night ahead of them, now that we've eaten we should go."

"But what about desert?" Rodger asks from the kitchen and everyone laughs.

"We can make our own dessert when we get home, honey, let's leave this one to them," Marianna says to him as she grabs his hand and leads him away from the cinnamon rolls.

With many hugs and much laughter everyone leaves, and Xanthe slowly makes her way into the elaborate bedroom Kiera's designed for her. The flowy white curtains on the window match those on the bed frame. Everything has a delicate green vine print on it and pictures of the house in the alps adorn the walls. On the nightstand next to my side of the bed is a framed wedding photo from Adam and Kiera with a note under it that says 'it's worth the risk'.

With a sigh, I flop down on the huge bed and grudgingly admit it's a lot more comfortable than the old mattress on the floor. I close my eyes, hands folded on my stomach, as I feel Xanthe crawl on the bed. Suddenly my face grows hot as Xanthe's soft skin surrounds me and I smell the sweetness of her center as she lowers it over my mouth. My eyes fly open and I grip her thighs instinctively as she sits on my face with her whole weight.

"I believe you said this morning you wanted to see how long I could ride your face? It's lucky you don't need to breathe because I have stamina you can't compete with." She smiles at me but her face quickly goes from seduction to shock as I lick her from the back all the way up. I live for the moans she makes when I eat her, but nothing is better than the gasp she makes when I sink my cock all the way in for the first time that session.

I've learned a lot from our past experiences, but what she doesn't know is all the studying I've done on my own. I watch as she realizes I've learned new tricks and relish as her whole body trembles in delight. I suck her clit, using the tip of my tongue to make light circles around the point of pleasure. She cries out, and much to her surprise, she comes, her body writhing and shuddering in the most delicious way. I growl as I lap up the flood of her juices, digging my nails into her thick thighs and continuing my efforts without a moment for her to relax.

"My...god...Brec," she gasps "My...turn...come...too fast..." She flings herself forward, grabbing the headboard and grinding my face wildly. For a moment I wish I could breathe, I wish she was suffocating me, because to die this way would be a hero's death and I'd go down in history. With a roar, I push her off my face and stand up on the bed so fast she doesn't even realized I'm not sucking her clit until my cock is all the way inside her and fucking her wildly.

I can't help it, I told her I'd let her ride me until she couldn't anymore but I need her now. She laughs as she sees I've shredded my clothes in an effort to be inside her as fast as possible, but she pulls away from me and gets off the bed.

"It's time to learn something new, Brec. Slow is also good."

She walks away from me and it's all I can do not to whine. My cock is hard and throbbing so bad it hurts. I follow her like a lovesick dog and she makes me sit on a love seat that wasn't here before. I reach for her, positively begging, and watch in awe as she climbs onto my lap and lowers herself onto my cock. I grab her hips, desperate to buck wildly, but she slaps my hands away.

"Don't make me tie you up, you know I would love to arrest you for what you've done..." she says quietly, her voice heavy and husky as she very slowly rocks against my cock.

She throws her head back and I lick her chocolate nipples. I fight every instinct in my body to stay still and let her take her pleasure, and the longer I do the better it feels.

The way she moves on my body is intoxicating, the slow undulation of her hips is a feeling like I could have never imagined. In my chest I feel something stir, a great welling feeling rising up my throat and fighting to come out my mouth.

I love her. I want to scream it, I want to tell the world. This is Xanthe and I love her more than any woman I've ever known.

"Mmm, your cock is going to be so hard to give up..." she moans and my heart drops.

That's right, she isn't mine. This is all a ruse to get my family to leave me alone. In a few short days she'll be gone, out of my life for good. Even though my heart is breaking, the sensation is too much and I fill her with waves and waves of my seed. The victory on her face is mesmerizing and I want to remember every second of this short time I have with her.

CHAPTER 9
XANTHE

"Brec, I don't think I'm ready..." I say, fidgeting with my white sundress and matching sandals.

A woman had come in and done my hair up in fancy braids and my curls fall artfully beside my face. I look like an angel, and Brec? He looks like a dark angel preparing for battle in a three-piece black suit. Tonight is the night I meet the rest of the family, so I need to look like the bride they think I am. All day I've been feeling more and more anxious, my heart giving me more trouble than usual. I've had to take more than my prescribed dose of analgesics.

I've got really close with Kiera over these last few days, and meeting the humans, Roger, Marianna and Mateo, that are important to them last night was amazing. It's getting harder and harder to imagine leaving Brec, walking away from this life, disappointing everyone.

Brec straightens his tie in the mirror and comes to sit next to me on the bed. "You have nothing to worry about, kitten. Everyone will love you just like Adam and Kiera do. You're basically part of the family already." He kisses my forehead and stands up, grabbing my shawl and waiting for me at the door.

"But I'm not." I start walking towards him and let him wrap me in the lace shawl. "I'm not part of your family, this is all pretend."

"What if it's not?" Brec asks, his voice shaking slightly.

"What do you mean? You set this up! You know I'm not...the one." I bite my bottom lip, tears welling up in my eyes. I can't be his Forever Bound. Life just can't be that cruel. I can't stay with him, no matter how much I want to.

"Crazier things have happened, look at Adam and Kiera. He hired her to find his Forever Bound, and then they discovered she *is* her." He grabs my hand and leads me towards the elevator.

"This isn't a fairy tale, Brec. It's a tragedy," I whisper.

He either doesn't hear or chooses not to listen. I barely recognize my surroundings as we leave the elevator and go to my Jeep and I don't object when Brec slips me into the passenger seat. The world is blurring through tears I'm trying not to shed. I told myself I wouldn't develop feelings, I promised myself this was just fun, just sex! It's all too real now, and I have to fight the urge to turn and run.

As we drive down the road, I try to imagine what an ancient castle full of vampires might look like. I stare out the window at the trees as they race by, and I think I see someone in the woods riding parallel to us.

I blink, rub my eyes, and it's still there.

The figure bursts from the trees, a woman in black leather on a motorcycle. She turns her head and looks at me, her mirrored helmet reflecting back my own terrified face as she raises a semi-automatic rifle and opens fire.

I scream and duck, glass shattering and tires screeching. Brec tries to cover my body with his and the jeep swerves out of control. In a flash, all I can see is shadows as the whole world goes dark. My stomach swoops somewhere to my feet as everything becomes a vague blur.

Somewhere behind me, there's the sounds of crashing and crunching metal and a woman curses. The preternatural movement stops and when the shadows clear, I'm standing alone in the middle of the road, covered in cuts and bruises.

The shadow is in front of me fighting the woman in leather, a bleeding shadow.

"Run! Xanthe! Silver bullets!" Brec screams, and the woman starts throwing silver knives into the mass of undulating black.

I look around frantically, my heart painfully thudding, wanting to run, wanting to help Brec. Miles down the road, high on the hill, the castle looms. More shadows burst from it, dark and wild. One shoots ahead, faster than the others, with lightning striking all around.

I look back to Brec, too scared to move as the woman in leather jumps on his back and suddenly I can see him clearly again. He looks at me, his eyes full of sorrow, and turns away as she runs the knife across his throat.

I'm screaming, I can hear it, but it's like it's not coming out of my mouth. I watch myself run at the fight, and I see myself jump on the woman in leather and rip her helmet off. She tosses me to the side and Brec slumps to the ground, lifeless.

"What are you doing, you idiot!" the woman snaps at me.

She turns to look at me and I'm rendered speechless. She's tall, very tall, with long straight slicked black hair in a high ponytail. Her bright blue eyes are fierce and angry, and her full lips are stretched over her teeth as she screams at me. "I'm trying to save you, half-wit! Get up, let's go!"

She storms towards me and I scramble back, my elbows and knees bloodied.

"Stay away from me!" I scream at her as I scramble to my feet.

She lunges at me and I dart away, avoiding her while trying to get close to Brec. The blood around him is pooling more and more, if I don't get there soon...

I duck and slide across the road as she tries to grab me again, slipping in Brec's blood as I roll him over. He looks at me, his eyes full of sorrow and fear, and clutches me. I instantly put pressure on his slit throat, it doesn't look like it got the carotid artery. He's riddled with bullet holes too and the familiar clenching pain as I think the person I'm trying to save won't survive washes over me.

The biker woman grabs me by my braids, pulling me back. "You're glamoured, but trust me, he's going to kill you!" she shouts at me.

I scream and thrash, willing to rip out all my hair to get back to Brec. He needs pressure on his wound!

"You're going to let her go if you know what's good for you..." a new voice threatens, and the woman wraps her arm around my waist and points a gun at my head.

"Don't worry," she whispers. "They won't let me hurt you, we'll get away."

"You're already hurting me, bitch! Let me go!" I keep struggling until I see Kiera materialize out of the storm shadows and bite her wrist, feeding Brec her blood.

Adam materializes next to her, and storms forward with two other men by his side. An older man, with silvering temples who must be their father, and a younger man. The younger man is wild, feral, baring his teeth and crouching low to the ground.

"Let my sister go, assassin..." he snarls.

On a normal occasion he might look half decent, dressed in a white button up shirt and black slacks. His hair looks like it was slicked back before he went all danger shadow and came to the rescue.

"She's innocent, vampire! I will save her from a needless

death!" the assassin shouts back, and lightning shoots from Kiera's hand as she rises and walks towards us.

"If you don't let my sister go and I have to fry you where you stand," Kiera threatens, sparks flying from her fingertips as she levitates off the ground.

Suddenly, the other brother is a shadow and jumping behind us. The assassin is distracted by Kiera and doesn't see the quick movement. He rips her off of me and bullets fly by my head. I duck, trembling, screaming, and Kiera is over me in a second.

I hear the motorcycle rev to life and look over my shoulder. The assassin is escaping, but the brother is on her heels. I'm still screaming, I can't stop. I barely register Brec sit up and reach for me, or Kiera kneel in front of me. Nothing comprehends until two strong hands grab my face from behind and force me to look at Kiera.

"Xanthe..." Kiera sings my name, and a strange heaviness comes over me, a forced calm. The hands on my face loosens and I brace my shoulders as Kiera gets closer. Adam must be holding me down. "Xanthe, you're safe now, she's gone. Brec is fine, see?"

She looks away and Adam turns my head, I see Brec walking over to me, wiping blood off his now scarred neck. My heart is beating out of control, it hurts so much. I clutch my chest and fold over in the fetal position and start to hyperventilate.

"Xanthe?" Brec shrieks, and he pushes his brother away from me and picks me up. "My love, are you alright? Xanthe?"

"You...love...me?" I whisper, just before everything goes black.

When I wake later, I realize that hours must have passed. I'm in what looks to be a hospital room but also a 15th century gothic castle. I sit up in bed and something stirs in a dark corner. The wild brother, now calm and collected. He walks towards me and sits on the edge of the bed.

"Sister..." he says, his eyes downcast. "I didn't catch her, she got away. I will make it my life's mission to make her pay. I swear this to you." He bows to me, actually bows, and then he stands and walks towards the door. "Brec is with Father, I'll let him know you have awakened."

I'm trembling, shaking, goosebumps all over my skin from head to toe. Sister? Father? As if he's my father too? I struggle out of bed, wincing at the soreness as scabs break open and leak a small amount of blood. I'm in a hospital gown, my clothes are gone. I scramble around the room looking for something, anything, to wear so I can get out of here.

"Xanthe?" Brec's breathy sigh of relief stops me in my tracks.

I look at him, alive, and all thoughts of running disappear. The thought of losing him overwhelms me I start sobbing uncontrollably.

His arms are around me before I can hit the floor and I cling to him like he's my life raft in a storm. He's kissing me everywhere; my face, my eyes, my lips. He sees my wounds and bites his wrist, forcing it against my mouth.

"Drink, my love. It will heal you." I do as I'm told, my whole body shuddering. I start feeling better almost instantly and Brec picks me up like a child and takes me to the bed. He strips my gown off, looking over every inch of me as I heal right before my eyes.

"Your blood would be useful in the hospital..." I joke weakly. "Maybe I should make you replace the bag you stole."

"Take a bag, take it all. Anything. I couldn't protect you, I almost lost you!" He crushes me against his chest and my heart spasms painfully.

"We had a deal, Brec." I start to push him back and he lets me, confusion on his face. "We said a week of sex just to trick your family. You didn't say anything about a cease fire, about assassins! She was trying to save me...from you... why would she do that? Who is she?"

Brec takes a deep breath, not letting his hands leave my legs. "No, I haven't told you the full truth because I never thought it would come to this. I thought I could fool my family and then disappear and they would never know. I never expected this to happen; to be attacked, to fall in love..." He leans forward to kiss me and I roll off the bed.

I stand there, naked in the moonlight, trembling. "You...you broke our understanding. You don't get to love me." Almost losing him has shown me exactly how deep I am. How much my feelings have grown a life of their own.

Feelings I can't afford to have.

I glance around the monstrous room frantically. "I-I'm leaving. Where are my clothes? This deal is void. Where are my clothes, Brec?" The last sentence comes out as a desperate shriek, and he jumps off the bed and tries to come to me but I back away, running towards the window and trying desperately to open it.

"I didn't sign up for assassins, war, I just wanted some good sex before...that doesn't matter, let me out of here!" I turn to him, tears running down my cheeks, and freeze.

Brec, the all-powerful, unstoppable vampire, is on his knees, head in his hands, crying.

"I'm so sorry, Xanthe... I never should have done this to you, but you are the one, you are my Forever Bound!" He looks at me, eyes desperate and breaking my heart.

I sob into my hand, leaning against the floor to ceiling windows. "No, no, I'm not. That's simply not possible..."

CHAPTER 10
BREC

Xanthe crumbles against the window, falling in a heap and sobbing. She says it can't be possible, but I can see my whole future in her eyes. I crawl over to her, taking her hands in mine. "Tell me how to fix this, I'll do anything. Please stay with me..." Never in my life have I asked for anything, much less begged, but I'd turn back time and not come to the castle tonight like she begged me not to do.

"There's nothing you can do. I have to go, this isn't fair..."

"Fair? Fair to who? You're leaving me, I've never felt love like this in centuries and you're leaving because it's not fair? Xanthe, I'll give you the world, I'll buy you anything you want, you'll never have to know hunger or pain again. I'll be forever loyal, we'll start a family—"

"No!" Xanthe shouts, ripping her hands away from me and pushing me away.

I can't help myself, my face hardens and shadows form around me. She can't leave me! She's mine!

Then I see the terror in her eyes and I realize she's not just scared, she's scared of me. I jump up, stepping away.

"You can go...after my week is up," I tell her, my voice is harder than it means to be. The thought of losing her is terrifying.

"Your week is void!" she shouts back at me, standing up and storming towards me. "You developed feelings I can't afford!"

"If you stay..." I start, I don't want to use this as an ultimatum but it's the last desperate straw I have. "If you stay for the rest of the week, I'll pay for state of the art medical care for Mara."

She faces me in a flash, her eyes blazing with anger and desperation. What she doesn't know is that I've already done it. Since the first day I saw what Mara meant to her, I've been working with Corbett investigating the best treatments possible.

"If you're lying..." she starts, a hint of deadly warning in her voice.

"I would never lie to you. I'll do everything I can to assure she survives this."

"Fine."

"Fine?" I ask, not having expected the response to be so quick.

"Fine, I'll stay. Just for the week, and no longer. Fall out of love, and let me go when it's over. You have to promise!" She walks towards me, desperation and longing in her eyes despite what she's asking of me.

"Why? Why only this week? Why won't you let me love you? I won't change you, I swear. We can run away after this week. Live anywhere in the world. You make me feel alive after centuries of existing. Why would you throw this connection away?"

"You'd never understand, Brec. So just drop it." She draws in a shaky breath, then flicks her mane of curls over her shoulder.

"Now, what's on the schedule for tomorrow? And when can you start the new treatment for Mara?"

"Treatment will start immediately." It started days ago, that's why she had the complications. "Tomorrow you will formally meet my family and we will tell them we plan on going away for your transformation, to protect you," I finish, and she laughs.

She laughs because now it's obvious she needs protection.

"Alright then," she says, suddenly looking exhausted. "I'll see you in the morning. I'll need clothes."

"I'm staying with you, Xanthe, I will not leave your side." I walk to her, my hand on her elbow as she tries to hide that she's crying.

I pull her against me, her back to my chest, wanting to be there for her even if I don't understand what's happening or why. She can sob for as long as she needs. I'm not going anywhere.

Except she struggles to get away from me. I let her, my heart aching for her, and she turns and slaps me across the face.

"How dare you!" she shouts, tears streaming down her face. "How dare you love me! How dare you do this!" She pounds my chest with her fists and I pick her up and throw her on the bed, laying over her and pinning her hands down.

"I do love you!" I shout over her tears and screams of frustration. "I love your light, I love your darkness. I love how much you love and I even love that you lie to me about it. I love you, I love you, I love you...and there's nothing you can do to change it. I will let you go, if that's what you want, but I will never stop loving you until the day I die."

Her heart is skipping beats again, like it does when she's aroused, so I kiss her gently. She sobs into my mouth but she doesn't fight me. Her lips tremble as she returns my kiss.

I loosen my grip on her arms and they wrap around my neck, her legs spreading automatically as she loses control. It takes but a slight shift of movement to free myself from my pants and slip inside her. She gasps, the way she does every time, and I love her more. "I love how your heart beats go crazy when I'm inside you..." I mumble against her neck and she sobs again, but I grab her hip and slowly push in and out. I took note of how she moved last time on the couch, and I angle my hips so I penetrate her just the way she likes.

She gasps, holding her breath, her nails digging into my back. I smirk, proud that I'm doing it right. I lean up slightly, adjusting so I hit her cervix every time. Something Adam told me makes them go wild. Her tears are forgotten, her eyes closed in utter pleasure.

When she opens them, she traces the bullet hole scars from the silver bullets, and leans up to kiss the scar on my neck. The gentleness almost makes me choke back a sob of my own.

"You can't touch me like that and tell me you don't love me in the same sentence..." I stop thrusting, my hands in her hair and our eyes locked. "You can't accept me like this, and look at me like that, and tell me in the same breath that you don't feel the same way I do. You are my Forever Bound, Xanthe, admit it..."

She's so beautiful, ethereal, as she lays beneath me, fresh tears streaming down her face, and she leans up and kisses me, rocking her hips against my cock so I have no choice but to thrust on instinct.

"Just...fuck me like it's the last time..." she begs, her arms tight around my neck and her body writhing underneath me.

"It's not the last time, Xanthe. I could do this every day for the rest of your life. When you die, I'll go with you. I'll end my life and follow you into the next. I love you, tell me you love me... tell me the truth."

She doesn't say it. She moans and rocks against me until she comes and she slowly drifts off to an exhausted sleep before I can finish.

I curl up next to her, cradling her in my arms and listen to her quiet snoring. I will not drift off tonight, I will stay awake and aware and protect her until my last breath. Heavens help anyone who seeks to steal her from me.

I will find a way to convince her to stay.

Daylight breaks the darkness too soon, and I grab my cell phone and text Kiera, asking her to send a servant with clothes and food for the both of us. I haven't so much as pressed send when servants waltz into the room, pushing racks of clothes and tables of steaming food.

"Coffee?" Xanthe sits bolt upright in bed, surprising me.

She's still stark naked and baring her breasts for all of them to see. I roar at them, throwing my body over Xanthe as they scatter in a hurry.

"I. Need. Coffee," Xanthe growls from beneath me, pushing on my chest as hard as she can.

As soon as the door closes, I slide off of her and she flies out of the bed faster than I thought possible. She runs to the table, finds the metal tin full of coffee, and melts into a chair as she pours it into a mug.

"French vanilla? Kiera remembers being human for sure!" She pours the creamer into her coffee and takes a deep breath through her nose. She sits back in the chair, kicking her feet as she takes a sip. "Don't look at me like that, I haven't had coffee since you snatched me from the hospital!"

"Knock knock! Hurry up, lovebirds! Dress and eat, Father is waiting in the library—I mean throne room!" Adam calls through the door.

Ever since he found Kiera, there's been no need for the library so he let Father claim it for its intended purpose. We eat quickly and dress, unfortunately all that was delivered was white lacy dresses for her and black suits for me. Clearly they expect to begin where we were meant to yesterday.

Kiera slips into a form fitting lace gown, low cut and baring her breasts much too much for a meeting with my family. I scowl at her and she cocks an eyebrow, daring me to say something. I roll my eyes and take her arm, leading her out of the room.

The throne room is massive without all the books, and on the dais there's a gilded chair for everyone, including Xanthe and me. I lead her up the stairs, noting the cracked place where Adam and Kiera had a bit too much fun and I smirk at Adam.

Adam stands with Kiera, beaming with pride as he takes note of where my glance is, and they meet us at the bottom of the stairs. Kiera takes Xanthe's hands from me and kisses her knuckles. "Welcome to the family, sister."

Kiera beams at Xanthe and my love only blushes and nods in response.

My father stands. "Welcome, my newest daughter! May your union bring strength to the family and bear many children!"

The applause is deafening, even the servants are clapping. Kiera turns, beaming at everyone in their thrones, and goes to walk back up the stairs but slips. She falls, landing right in the spot they broke before, and marble goes flying.

Xanthe, always fast in an emergency, drops to her knees and holds Kiera's head in her lap. Kiera blinks, looks around, and screams. Blood starts pouring from between her legs in a flood, and Xanthe's eyes go wide with shock.

"Be calm, my children," my father roars above the din of panic. "She's going into labor. A vampiric baby does not nestle in water. A vampiric child floats in blood."

CHAPTER II

XANTHE

"Does she even know what she's doing?" Adam scowls as we rush Kiera to the hospital style room I slept in the night before.

"It's either you let Xanthe help or watch Kiera suffer while we wait for the doctor. Make your decision," Brec bites back.

I hear nothing of their disagreement, not really. I'm completely focused on Kiera. No one knows my past, and for good reason. I don't let people in. But right now what I want and what Kiera needs are at odds, and Kiera is more important than my privacy.

We get to the room and I help Kiera onto the bed. She's in agonizing pain, I can tell, but she's doing her best not to scream. Her eyes are bulging, her lips thin and bared over her teeth. When Zarius, the family's patriarch, tries to push his way through the door, Kiera finally lets out her first scream.

"Out! All of you men! Leave me with Xanthe, go now!" she wails, her strength growing as her silver storm shadows begin to fill the room.

I have to smile at Kiera's strength, she's more formidable

than any woman in labor I've ever witnessed. She grabs the headboard, crouching on the bed and bearing down.

"You're doing amazing, Kiera. Listen to your instincts. That's right!" I climb on the bed with her, putting a steadying hand on her shoulder. The shadows around us spark as she grows more and more scared and the pain continues to ebb and flow through her body. "Kiera, I need to touch you, examine how far along you are."

All she can do is nod. I lean into her and she drops her head on my shoulder as I reach down to examine her.

I freeze and Kiera shrieks. "What is it? What's wrong with my baby?"

"She...she's holding my hand...she's pulling."

I'm in complete shock, there's a tiny hand wrapped around my index finger with immense strength. I lay down on my back to get a better view, discovering a white mist is pouring from inside Kiera. The color is startling next to all the blood. There's one hand out, clutching mine, and pulling.

"Kiera, when I tell you to, you must push. Your baby is eager to join you, but she needs your help." I look up at Kiera and she nods fast, once, and focuses on something in the distance.

"Is it safe? Her hand being out first?" Kiera has to stifle a sob, fear overwhelming her pain.

"I've never delivered a vampire baby before, but she's strong, she won't let me go. The strength is phenomenal. She has a white mist, Kiera. I feel like I'm watching the birth of an angel...now push!"

Kiera does, screaming so loud the glass on the floor to ceiling windows crack and the men burst through the doors in a panic.

The child's head is out, her bright blue eyes focused on me, and another arm reaches out and grabs my hand. I cradle her back and turn her around, face up. Never in my life have I seen a baby who looks at me with such intensity. She doesn't cry, as if she's determined. Kiera lets out one last, piercing cry and the rest of the child slides out.

The room goes completely white with mist. I fall back on the bed, cradling the bloody child to my chest as Kiera sobs.

"Is she alright? I can't see anything! Why isn't she crying?" Kiera is shrieking, panic setting in, as the men try to battle the white mist with their own black shadows and fail.

Slowly the mist clears around the baby's face and I look into eyes too intelligent to be real. She's ethereal, beautiful. Her hands wrap around my fingers and she smiles, showing perfect little fangs in an otherwise gummy mouth.

"She's...perfect..." I mumble, in sheer disbelief. "Sweet baby, you must clear the mist, your mother is waiting for you."

The exquisite child coos at me and the mist begins to lower to the floor and dissipate. I rise to my knees in front of Kiera, who's collapsed on the bed, tears streaming down her beautiful face. The whole room goes quiet in sheer awe as I hand Kiera the baby over the bed covered in blood.

"My sweet girl..." Kiera sobs as she takes her, and they lock eyes. "Umm, is this normal? She's looking right at me!"

"I have...no idea..." I say between gasps for breath.

My heart is beating wildly, out of control. I'm covered in blood and mucus from the birth and my hands are shaking. The men surround the bed. Adam is crying, Brec steadies my shoulders, and Zarius throws his head back with a victorious laugh.

"Such overwhelming strength! Such a presence of power! A valkyrie born to my family, blood of my blood!" he declares.

Brec eases me off the bed, hugging me tightly as he watches his new niece latch on Kiera's breast. Blood pools in the corners of the baby's mouth.

"She's not biting, I'm lactating blood!" Kiera says, her voice hushed with astonishment. The sweet baby reaches up and grabs a lock of her mother's hair, pulling gently as they stare into each other's eyes and form an unbreakable bond. I can't help it, I'm crying. I turn to face Brec and sob into his chest. I've always loved children and after seeing this birth, the knowledge that I will never have my own burns me alive.

The cracked windows suddenly shatter as black and silver wings spiral through the room, causing sharp fragments to scatter everywhere. Brec spins and curls around me, protecting me from the glass storm. Peeking past his arm, I stare in shock as a literal black winged angel appears at Kiera's bedside.

"My child..." the angel coos, and every man in the room launches into battle.

Fierce eyes turn on them and they all freeze in place. I find I'm the only one who can move, so I throw myself over Kiera and the baby.

"I don't know who you are, but you will not harm my family!" I scream, ready to die for Kiera and the baby.

"You, human, can withstand my power?" She looks at me with something close to disgust and grabs me by the throat, hanging me so my feet just brush the floor. I thrash and kick and scream as Kiera looks up in absolute terror.

"Mother, please, don't...don't hurt her...I'm begging you..." Kiera sobs, clutching the baby to her chest.

Mother? This dark angel is Kiera's mother? I kick and struggle, trying my best to strike this woman, but she bats me with her wings and my vision fades. It takes everything in me not to fall unconscious. The angel's free hand reaches out and strokes the baby's soft brown hair and the child turns and hisses at her. She sees me, thrashing, and anger fills the tiny baby's eyes.

In a flash of white, a heavy fog fills the room, pushing the angel back and away. "What is this?" I hear her scream.

She's pulling me with her. In mere moments, the unfettered

breeze of being outside several floors up in the air brushes my skin.

"Xanthe!" I hear Brec scream.

The mist in the room clears, the men are free from whatever the angel did to them, and I look up at her as we float freely in the air.

"You delivered the child," she says to me, not a question, a statement.

I try to nod but she tightens the grip on my throat. Brec is racing towards the window as Adam throws himself over the child and his wife. Zarius is dark with shadow as he takes a silver lance from Mateo, who's appeared in the doorway like magic.

"She's very powerful...this cannot stand," the dark angel holding me snarls. "I will be back for my daughter, and my granddaughter. The cease fire ends on this day."

The patriarch of the Cadells throws his lance at us, and the angel drops me. The lance nicks her wing and she screams as blackness envelops me and I suddenly feel solid marble under my feet again.

"You could have killed my mate!" Brec shouts as clattering and shattering furniture scatters everywhere.

He puts me down and Brec and Adam fly through the door, attacking their father, rage and blood flying. The fight quickly moves out of the room and I sag against a wall. Breathless, the sound of fighting fading in the castle, I look at Kiera. She reaches for me, and feeling boneless, I go to her side.

"Who was that?" I ask, sitting on the bed next to her and reaching for the baby, who takes my hand and chews on my finger.

"My mother, the matriarch of our enemy coven, the Monroes," Kiera mutters in shock. "I always wanted my mother to be at my bedside when I had my baby." She chuckles, wiping sweat from her forehead. "But the mother I knew died when I was little. That woman is nothing but a monster trying to destroy my family."

"I don't think this little girl is going to let that happen." I stroke the dark down of her hair and I swear the newborn baby smiles at me. White mist curls around my arm like a serpent, an embrace, as both Kiera and I are surrounded in a cloud of pearl. The cloud is so dense, all sounds of fighting are blocked out. It's like Kiera and I and the sweet baby are in another world.

"Genevieve... I will call her Genevieve, after my Babushka," Kiera whispers.

The baby coos in delight.

"Ginny for short? How precious..." I lean in and kiss the little girl's head.

"You must make the transition soon, my sister," Kiera says, and I look up at her in shock. She takes my hand with her free one and pulls it to her lips, kissing my knuckles gently. "This world is too dangerous for a human, and I couldn't bear to lose you. Please, tell Brec it's worth the risk. We can all see your destiny."

I swallow a lump in my throat as the mist begins to dissipate and the men return, looking rough and bruised but laughing. Whatever happened, they seem to have worked it out.

The next day a party is declared; Genevieve will be blessed by all the members of the Cadell clan and their followers. Servants I have yet to see fill the halls, and everyone is dressed in finery like I could only imagine in books. My hair is twisted around a silver tiara and my dress is silver and body hugging. Walking toward the throne room, I feel so exposed, every detail of my shape is visible. I'm wearing diamonds more expensive than I could imagine and my face is beet red as everyone stares in awe.

As if some blessing is bestowed on me, my phone begins to ring. I slip into a room and go stand out on the balcony, desperately needing a breath of fresh air. Clouds are rolling in from the south over the city and it looks like rain. I pull my phone out of a clutch that matches my dress, registering an unknown number. Shrugging, I answer it anyway. Any excuse to stay out here longer.

"Xanthe..."

My breath stutters at the familiar voice. One I shouldn't be hearing.

"How did you get this number, Xavier?" I snap at my brother.

I cut my whole family off long ago. Told them to consider me dead, burned my bridges. I didn't want anyone to see me fade.

"You're in danger, Xanthe. I taught you how to take care of yourself better than this," Xavier says, his voice dark and angry.

"The only thing you taught me is abandonment. Which, by the way, you taught me well. Lose my number, and don't contact me ever again!" I shout, going to hang up.

"I refuse to let you die with them, Xanthe," Xavier warns, and I hear a gasp behind me.

"Who is that? What are they talking about?" shouts a voice.

I turn around quickly to see Brec standing there, his face contorted in rage and despair. He snatches the phone out of my hand as I stare at him with my mouth open, unable to answer.

"Who are you?" Brec roars into my cell.

"Cadell, you will release my sister. She does not have time to waste pretending to be your mate. Release her to me, or all the might of the Monroes will crash down on this little party of yours," I hear my brother threaten and my knees go weak.

"A Monroe minion, are you?" Brec snarls. "You will not threaten my mate, she's not going anywhere!"

"So you're content to watch her fade away and die for your ruse? I knew your clan was selfish, but this is next level. Release her to me, I'll make her get chemo. If you actually love her, you'll let her go." Xavier's words come out like a hiss, and I can imagine him clenching his teeth as he speaks.

Brec looks at me, his eyes hollow. "Chemo?" he mutters in disbelief.

"You're a vampire, Cadell, you can't tell me you can't hear her heart falter," Xavier snarls. "Angelica knew her mere moments before she figured it out, before she told me where my sister was. She's dying, and there's nothing you can do to save her. She's not your Forever Bound, she's a sick desperate woman who pushes everyone who loves her away. Let her go, Cadell. Give her a chance to live."

Brec walks deeper into the room, black shadows pouring out of him like ink over the floor. "She's my Forever Bound, I'll prove it here and now! I'll drain her, she will become a vampire and there will be no need of chemotherapy, I—"

My scream breaks Brec's declaration.

The sound of flapping wings bursts behind me, and as I turn to face the noise, a flock of winged vampires close in around me.

One of them grabs me, pinning my arms to my sides, and kicks off the balcony, flying away. Through the wings I can hear Brec roar, the shadows filling the room and surrounding the vampires there to fight him.

The one carrying me flies away, surrounded by torrents of other vampires.

They're moving so fast I can't even catch a breath.

Oblivion is inevitable.

CHAPTER 12

BREC

Wings everywhere, slapping my face as claws gnash at my skin. I fight wildly, desperately, I can't hear Xanthe anymore. Even as I can hear the man on the phone laughing, absolutely evil. Without a weapon and in a dress suit, my only defense is my shadows and sheer strength. I duck and weave, trying to evade the onslaught as the door crashes open and my brothers fill the room.

The battle rages on, bloody and brutal. I'm given a sword and I hack and slash at the enemy. Wings are severed as well as limbs, the Monroe vampires dropping like flies. Very few escape the room alive, everyone mortally wounded.

The moment I can, I run for the balcony. Standing there, covered in carnage, I search the skies for any glimpse of Xanthe.

But she's gone.

I turn, furious, and look at all the dead bodies and my bloodied brothers.

Devion, in for the ceremony, grabs one vampire and slices his wings off as he tries to escape. The vampire screams, and Devion turns him around and holds them to his chest with his blade to their throat.

"This one we keep alive for questioning...what fun I will have with you!" Devion licks the terrified vampire's face and he screams.

I storm forward, my silver blade poised over the enemy's heart. "Where is she?" I demand.

"With her brother..." The enemy sputters through the blood foaming at his lips. His eyes are wide with fear even as he laughs in my face. "You truly think we would let you get another bride? Ha! He will watch her die in the dungeons before we let you gain even more power. One that can resist Angelica? Too risky!" He laughs and Devion slits his throat lightly enough for blood to spurt but not damage his vocal cords.

"Where did they take her?" I scream in his face, my sword inching towards his heart.

The man is crazed, wild, with no care for his own self. He laughs as I push, prepared to inflict as much pain as is needed, but before I can plunge my sword through his chest a white mist fills the room.

Kiera walks in with Ginny on her hip, the child has grown so much overnight that she can hold herself up and look around. "Ginny told me she needs to see him..." Kiera whispers, her face white with shock. "She said it...in my mind."

She walks around my brothers, her storm clouds thundering as fear rolls through her. She stands between me and the prisoner, then places her hand on the sword but doesn't push it away.

The Monroe vampire looks at Ginny and starts to scream, blood dripping from his eyes, finally full of nothing but fear. He arches in Devion's arms, fighting whatever onslaught he's experiencing, and clearly losing. The vampire goes silent with a squelch, and his body falls limp on the ground.

Kiera, breathing heavily, turns to me in utter shock. My mind fills with a picture, a home in the woods. A miniature castle. Xanthe is underground, deep underground. She's in the arms of a man who looks eerily like her, in the presence of Angelica and Thaddeus themselves.

My vision clears, and I falter back against a wall and slide to sit on the floor, pure shock taking over my senses.

"We all saw…" Adam mutters in awe.

"Xanthe has cancer in her heart," Kiera says, her eyes distant. It doesn't sound like her. The baby reaches for me and I stand and take her tiny hand in mine.

Save her… a tiny voice touches my mind.

"When I changed, all my wounds were healed, even old scars faded to nothing. Brec, she can be saved. We just have to get there in time," Kiera says, her voice her own again.

I look around at my father and brothers. "Once again, the Monroes have swept in to steal one of our women. Angelica has threatened Kiera and Ginny. How long will we let them interfere?" I demand, and my brothers rage and scream in agreement.

Our father leans back against the wall, nonchalant. "I've been telling you boys this for centuries, and only now do you take me seriously? The Monroes have to be eradicated. Assemble our armies, call everyone in. We will get Xanthe back, or we will burn the entire clan to ashes trying."

Everyone roars in agreement and the castle vibrates with the war cry. My brothers scatter to the four winds, calling to every vampire under our control, and soon the Cadell castle is swarming with so many men that the grounds look black with all the bodies assembled for battle. We stand on the stairs to the castle, addressing the masses.

Kiera's behind us, her baby clinging to her neck, and we declare open war.

The roar that rises around the castle echoes all the way to Sorin City, no doubt making the humans tremble with unknown fear and rushing to the safety of their homes. They wouldn't know why, only that it's time to hide. Like a muscle memory passed down from their ancestors, the streets will be clear.

"They have taken my mate!" I roar over the crowd, coming down the stairs. "They took her while she remains human, and the danger has never been greater. We must rescue her, but we must ensure no harm comes to her in our wake. She is underground here." I hold up a map and point to the spot where I know the smaller castle is. "Do no damage to the structure, she may be buried under rubble if you do. They may attempt to kill her rather than let her come back to us..." My voice trails off and I swallow hard.

Adam comes up behind me and puts his hand on my shoulder. "We have all seen the immense power of a vampiric woman, and the power of our offspring!" He looks at his wife and daughter, pride written all over his face. "We must get our sister back, strengthen our coven even more. Help us rescue our princess and we vow to help every man here find his own Forever Bound no matter how high or low you are in the clan rankings. We must bolster each other for the great battle to come. Are you with us?"

The roar that comes from the men is positively deafening.

Adam puts his arm around my shoulder and the royal family goes back into the castle as our soldiers scatter and prepare for battle. All around the din and clash of weapons can be heard, the donning of armor on every man is uproarious. My brothers and I dress in the black armor we have not worn in centuries, and Kiera puts on matching armor made just for her. Father and Adam will stay behind to protect her as Corbett, Devion, and Ever join me on the battlefield.

We gather in the throne room and Kiera takes the central throne with Ginny in her arms. The floor is covered with

Ginny's white mist and it swirls around our feet as we approach the thrones and bow to Kiera and the child.

"Save my sister," Kiera orders and all the men, including my father and the servants, bow to the matriarch of the Cadell clan.

Father has acceded his throne to her, and the sheer awe of her presence and the power of her child overwhelms everyone in the room. I watch as Adam goes up to his wife and stands at her side, hand on her shoulder. The painting of the royal family comes together before my eyes. The sheer strength emanating from this one couple is humbling, and I harden my heart for battle.

I know Xanthe will mirror this strength, and our children will be just as powerful as Genevieve.

Kiera nods at me, and I rise, walking up the dais to kneel at her feet. "Bring my sister back to me, so she will never be harmed again."

The fierceness in Kiera's eyes makes me tremble, and a bow of my head, I stand.

Leaving the room flanked by my brothers I feel a power roll over us, a blessing from the child, and as we leave the castle surrounded by a flood of black shadow our roar of battle tears through the night like a banshee's scream.

CHAPTER 13
XANTHE

When I wake, I'm lying on a rock table in a stone cell with my twin brother looking over me. He'd dyed my hair back to black while I was unconscious, and I look up into my mirror image and feel only rage. My silver dress is torn and frayed, my jewelry broken and diamonds scattered throughout the cell.

Xavier smiles down at me and I slap him as hard as I can across the face.

He staggers back and spits blood. "That's one way to thank me for saving you from being drained and discarded," he growls and storms towards me, forcing my shoulders down painfully onto the stone bed. "Dominique tried to save you and got chased off by those monsters. I succeed in saving you and you strike me! What is wrong with you? Are you truly so glamoured that not even Angelica's powers could touch you?" He shakes me, and I spit in his face.

"I told you when I was diagnosed that I would die on *my* terms. This was my choice, you had no right—"

"Silence, human," a woman's voice interrupts me and Xavier lets me sit up to face the leaders of the Monroe clan.

Their wings are tight to their backs, their faces a mirror image of rage. "You helped my daughter, so I will not let you be tortured, but I cannot risk you turning into a weapon for my enemy. Thaddeus, drain her," Angelica orders and Thaddeus steps forward.

But Xavier jumps between us. "No! You promised to help me save her! After I spent most of my life being your servant, this is how you repay me?" he cries, trying to protect me with his own body.

"The only thing that can save her from her fate is the man we just stole her from!" Angelica shouts.

Scalding tears track down my face. So it's true, Brec is my fated mate. The answer to my cancer, my salvation, my savior. Our first meeting flashes before my eyes as my brother is cruelly thrown aside. Thaddeus Monroe looms over me, and I'm frozen in fear.

"She's too powerful to risk us letting her change, finish her!" Angelica roars, her silver tipped wings spreading out behind Thaddeus to keep Xavier away from us.

I watch my brother battering uselessly against her as Thaddeus lifts me to sitting and slides behind me. His hands on my body makes my skin crawl, his touches seem sexual and his breath on my neck makes me want to be physically sick. His fangs pierce my neck and I scream, the sound echoes off the stone wall and reverberates.

I try to struggle. I try to fight. I finally have something worth living for!

But Thaddeus is too strong. His fangs pierce deeper, and the flow of my blood from my body to his mouth leaves my limbs feeling cold. Numb. He's sucking me dry.

Suddenly, the walls begin to shake, stones and dust falling everywhere, and Thaddeus stops feeding, looking around in shock.

Angelica wavers as the whole building shudders. Xavier's eyes are so wide, the white seems to dominate his face. Beyond the walls, the sound of battle can be heard as the ground rumbles with hundreds, if not thousands of men marching.

Angelica screams, and my head shoots to her. Devion has latched onto her back, ripping out her neck with his teeth. Thaddeus roars and throws me against the wall and rises, wings flaring, and attacks Devion.

They hit the opposite wall in a flurry of fangs and talons and I shake away the weakness and pain. This is my chance to get away.

I've just sat up when Angelica crawls over to me, blood gushing down her neck, yet baring her teeth in a deadly smile. I back up as far as I can but she grabs my ankle and pulls me across the floor to her. I cry out as she bites my neck, drinking greedily and I watch in horror as she begins to heal. My death will mean her survival.

Xavier roars, and a silver dagger crashes down on Angelica, slicing one of her wings wide open and rendering it useless. She screeches in pain and pushes herself off of me in a flash, her neck almost healed. Thaddeus is battling with Devion, and with one powerful roar and twist, Devion throws him bodily up the stairs.

I run to my brother and he wraps his arms around me. "I'm so sorry!" he sobs. "They said they would cure you, I had to try and save you! I'm so sorry!"

I cling to him, crying as blood runs from my neck on both sides. I can feel myself getting weak, fading, and my knees give out. Xavier hauls me against him, his strength the only thing holding me up. We both turn to face the furious vampiress wanting us dead.

But Angelica hisses at us and flees, running up the stairs after Devion and Thaddeus.

"Quick," Xavier pants. "We have to get out of here."

Escape it all I want. Brec's arms call to me. I want to see him one more time... But I can't move. My eyelids feel too heavy. Xavier places his arms under my legs and behind my head and carries me out of the dungeon.

The scene above ground is carnage, bodies of both vampire families litter the ground. The battle still rages above as well as on the ground, grunts and cries and the clash of weapons filling the air. I see the youngest brother, Ever, fall to the ground with a winged vampire on top of him.

"Help him, Xavier!" I shout, and Xavier sets me down and runs at the vampire.

His body slams him off of Ever right before Corbett descends to help. They quickly become a tangle of limbs and wings, a fine red mist rising above them.

Directly above me I see Devion and Brec, both attacking Thaddeus midair, their shadows supporting their weight. Behind a pile of rubble, Angelica appears and she flies into the sky weakly, using her power to freeze the Cadell men. They immediately crash to the ground. Thaddeus flies to his woman and supports her, both bleeding profusely.

"Retreat," he roars. "Retreat!"

I lay there, bleeding out as the Monroes flee and the Cadells follow. Ever is at my side in a flash, feeding me his blood so I can heal, but I can tell I've lost too much of my own already. I'm too weak to drink.

Seems death was my fate after all.

I fall limp in Ever's arms. For a vampire, he's young, his face still holding a childlike softness. I reach up and stroke his face and his eyes go wide as he sees I'm not healing.

"Brec! You must come! She's dying!" Ever screams as my vision blurs.

Brec's face appears above me and I almost smile. The last

thing I remember before everything fades to black is feeling my sick, failing heart swell with unending love.

When I wake I'm completely alone. I sit bolt upright in my bed as I realize I can't feel my heart beating. I begin to cry, looking around the beautiful gauzy white room, and seeing my white silk and lace gown. I'm healed, my hair wild and dark around my head, in an all-white room with a warm gentle breeze blowing through the open windows.

And I can't feel my heart.

"I'm dead!" I wail, falling back on the bed and crying into the soft pillows.

Dead, after everything, I'm dead. I left him alone on the battlefield and died and now I'm in some fluffy heaven. I deserve to be in hell for what I did to Brec. Letting him develop feelings for me was cruel!

"Shhh, you're not dead silly," a small child's birdlike voice sings to me.

Tiny hands touch my shoulder, and I turn to see a toddler on the bed with me. Her flowing brown curls frame her ice-blue eyes as she looks down at me, her face more angelic than a cherub. She touches my face, and my tears stop in their tracks.

"G-Ginny?" I stutter, and she nods.

"I told mommy to put you in my room while you heal. I dressed you up like a dolly! You're so pretty and perfect now, you look like a tan porcelain doll!" Ginny giggles and claps, bouncing on the bed.

I slowly sit up and look around again, seeing the large bed

I'm on and the crib and the toddler bed and the toys ranging from infant to child scattered around the room. Ginny throws her arms around my shoulders and squeezes so tight I feel like my neck will break.

"Uncie Brec didn't think you're gonna wake up, but I *told* him you would." She bounces on the bed as she hugs me, and my throat goes absolutely dry and aching. "Oh! Of course you're hungry, here!" She jumps off the bed and shouts out the door and a rumbling of footsteps shakes the bed beneath me.

My new family floods through the door, Brec leading them, and he takes me into his arms so fast and hard that I normally would have shattered bones. All I can feel is waves of pure love, his skin is like velvet on mine.

"You're awake!" His voice breaks as he speaks, kissing me everywhere and holding me so tight.

"We all told you she was the one!" Adam says from the doorway, a smile of victory on his face.

Behind him, Devion brings my brother in chains. Xavier's head is down, his body bruised and bloody, and a raging anger rips through me. Thunder clouds form around me as I shove Brec away and rise from the bed. Wind starts to rip apart the room as billowing tunnels form around me. My family looks around in sheer astonishment but not an ounce of fear. Devion pushes Xavier at me and takes two steps back.

"I'm sorry, Xanthe! Please forgive me," Xavier shouts over the tornadoes that are ripping the room apart around me, but nothing of the wind disturbs a hair on my family. I look at Ginny, who smiles and waves at me. She's protecting them. The winds batter my brother as he fights his way forward, and I use my newfound strength to shatter his bonds. He flies into me and I wrap my arms protectively around him, falling to the floor and leaning over him as the winds fade.

"I'm so sorry!" my brother sobs, pulling me to his chest, his whole body shaking. "Use me, Xanthe, feed off me. Feed yourself with my blood, let me sustain you," he begs, and I try to pull away but he holds me. I'm much stronger than him, so I freeze, worried I'll break his arms if I pull too strongly.

"I will not kill you!" I scream, the winds picking up again.

"You don't have to kill me, just sustain yourself!" He pushes his arm against my face and my instincts take over. I bite him, my eyes wide with shock, and as his blood fills my mouth, a euphoria I've never felt comes over me.

Brec comes up behind me, pulling me off my brother before I can drink too much. Blood drips from my mouth and I turn on him, absolutely starving. I bite him instantly, savagely, and the moan that comes out of him snaps me back to reality.

He tastes different, better, and the heady flavor of him sets me on fire. He pulls me hungrily against his body, laying me down on the floor, and bites me back. I thought my first taste of blood was euphoria, but this is an out of body experience. I barely notice that everyone leaves the room, Adam covering Ginny's eyes and Kiera helping my brother to his feet.

Before the door closes, my fingers turn to white talons and I rip Brec's clothes to shreds.

CHAPTER 14
BREC

Her body is like heaven, hard and strong like it never was before. Her soft curves now stand up to me squeezing them as hard as I can, and as she shreds my clothes she makes me go wild. I pull up the hem of her nightgown and feel how hot and wet she is between her thighs. I rub her clit as we bite each other, and her moans go from needy to raging mad.

Xanthe, now stronger than ever, pushes me off her and I fly across the room and shatter the glass windows and land on the balcony. She growls as she walks over, shredding her gown, and I stare up at my queen with awe and desire. She mounts me forcefully, plunging my pulsing cock inside her with zero fore-play. It's all I can do to hold on to her hips as she rides me wildly. She's taking pleasure from my body, holding me down so hard I couldn't move if I tried to.

I watch her, mind totally blank beside the pleasure and sheer love. Her body has changed, her black curls like a halo around her head with a fresh new life. Her tan skin glows like a tropical sunset, and her breasts and body look fuller than they ever have. As she rides me, completely ignorant to what's going on around her, it hits me just how sick she's been this whole time. Compared to now, she looked like she had one foot in the grave. Her vivacity is the same, but her strength is a hundredfold.

Her hot sheath tightens and spasms around me as she gets close to coming, and finally she looks down at me. When her eyes lock on mine, I know my fate is sealed. The love coming from her is undeniable, irrevocable, and as she comes the skies above her flash with lightning and let loose their rains. I watch the deluge wash her body, crystal water dripping off her hard nipples as she rocks with a feral rhythm. The lighting flashes, making her caramel skin glow as she orgasms, a vision of beauty and untamed power. She falls on me, replete, and as her passion ebbs so does the storm.

All around us a white mist rises, hiding us from any eyes around the castle. The only thing I can see is the love of my life and the full moon above her as she falls onto my chest. I stroke her back reverently and she kisses my neck tenderly. She nips my ear and laughs breathily.

"You didn't come, Brec," she whispers into my ear and I chuckle.

"I was too distracted by you and your pleasure to seek my own, my love," I tell her as she rises up, both hands on either side of my head.

"Take your pleasure now, or I will be most displeased," she says, her voice stern and demanding.

Without delay I stand up, carrying her with me, and set her on the marble railing of the balcony. She locks her legs around my waist and shrieks in sheer pleasure as I fuck her. She raises her arms above her head, floating in the mist with only my hands and cock keeping her from falling, but she feels no fear.

Her body is nothing like it was before, its sheer strength and power is blowing me away. As I fuck her, her abs tighten and loosen, her beautiful big breasts bobbing with every one of my powerful strokes. The way her cunt surrounds me and holds me inside her makes me feel absolutely drunk. Her shaft grips me in waves, starting at the base and rolling to the tip of my cock. I grunt, shocked and in pure awe, as she locks eyes with me and I fill her with my seed. Her own special brand of lightning crackles through my veins, making me gasp and roar, making me humble and strong all at once. Waves and waves of cum explode inside her as the pleasure grips me and doesn't let go.

It pours from me like she's pulling it out, every ounce I've ever made seems to fill her and drip out from our joining. Her victorious grin is almost as rewarding as the orgasm itself, and as my knees grow weak, I pull her to my chest and lower us to the floor. She doesn't release my cock, she gets on her knees and rides me still, and all I can do is look at her with all the love I've ever felt in the world. I kiss her chest, worshiping every inch of her skin, sucking on her breasts and biting her nipples to feed off her.

Her nails dig into me as she gets closer again, and I make up my mind to fill her as she comes on me. She rides me harder, and I reach behind myself supporting my body with my arms as I thrust my hips up into her. I feel my load coming, hot and hard, and as it explodes into her she tightens around me like a vise. Our combined screams of pleasure fill the night, and we ride each other until the waves of sheer bliss finally fade.

Afterward, I carry Xanthe like the queen she is to the bed in the room. I lay her down, laying behind her, and stroke every inch of her skin. She nestles against me, her body fitting against mine as if she was always meant to be there, and come to think of it, she was. Her hand covers mine and she pulls my palm to her stomach.

"I want a baby, Brec," she says, tears filling her eyes as her voice breaks. The sheer need to have a child is breaking her heart and mine.

"I'll give you a dozen babies, as many as you want. We can raise an army of just our children, I promise." I kiss her shoulder and she laughs quietly.

"My brother, can he stay? Without the chains?" she asks, turning to me as tears drop from her eyes onto the bed.

My throat gets tight, as if I could ever deny her? All I can do is nod. She smiles slyly and starts moving my hand down, down, until the combined wetness of our love making is soaking our fingers.

"If we're going to raise an army..." She sighs as my fingers slip inside her and find her g-spot automatically and she grinds against my hand. "We don't get to stop until I'm pregnant."

When we finally emerge from Genevieve's room, the place is absolutely destroyed. We walk out sheepishly, holding each other's hands, and nod at the servants who go in to clean up the mess without making eye contact. In the hall we pass Mateo and Xavier, who's been completely healed and talking to Mateo about the job they've both done for vampires for most of their lives. Apparently, Xavier was to the Monroes what Mateo is to us, but now his loyalties lie only with his sister.

We pass them with quick hugs and the astonishing information that we've been locked away in that room for a week.

Xanthe giggles under my arm as I lead her to the throne room and the room we enter is completely different than before. The walls are painted white, the books removed to put in rows of seating. The dais itself has been transformed, with two towering white thrones sitting next to each other and flanked by the ebony stones from before.

Kiera rises from one of the white thrones and runs to Xanthe, taking her hand and drawing her from me to show her the other throne. "This one's for you!" she says with a giddy smile as she insists that Xanthe sits down.

She sits on the throne next to her and waves at my brothers and I to take our seats. As we do, Adam by Kiera and myself next to Xanthe, the doors to the throne room open and humans and Cadell vampires alike pour in. They take their seats, mingled with one another, and wait patiently as a man in red robes walks up the center aisle and stands at the foot of the dais, then bows.

"I hear a wedding is in order?" he asks, bent over, his long beard touching the floor. Kiera jumps up and claps, grabbing Xanthe's hand and pulling her up into a hug.

"A double wedding!" she announces.

Now I know why there were such fine clothes waiting outside our door. Adam stands and takes Kiera's hand and nods at me to do the same. I rise, looking at Xanthe in all her vampiric glory.

Both women are positively glowing, and all our servants and family are clapping. It seems everyone knew but us. I stare at Xanthe, her white lacy gown that we joked was a bit much mere moments before now revealed as her wedding dress. I can't wait. I pull her against my chest and kiss her, only to be interrupted by the clearing of a throat.

"The damn priest hasn't said anything yet, boy! Show some patience!" Our father marches into the room, climbing the stairs to the dais and patting the priest's shoulder on the way. He stands between us and places a hand on both women's shoulders. "This is a glorious day! One I gladly relinquish my head of household name for!" he shouts over the roar of the crowd. "Two women have joined my family, and today we bind them in matrimony! Our power has grown triple from what it was with the two brides and the cherub they have delivered to me!"

Little Ginny runs out from the crowd and jumps into her grandfather's arms. I shouldn't be surprised, but she looks to be about five years old now.

"Never in the history of our clan have we been so powerful!" My father tickles little Ginny's side and smiles broadly at her. She lays her head on his shoulder and sticks her thumb in her mouth, watching the gathering quietly. "Today, I have asked all our human and vampire families alike to assemble and celebrate this joyous occasion! Your holiness, if you will." He nods to the priest and steps to the side, taking a large throne near the fireplace and bouncing Ginny on his knee.

"We are gathered here today," the priest begins as he climbs the stairs and stands between us and my brother and Kiera. "To join these two wonderful couples in holy matrimony..."

The rest of the service goes by in a blur, I repeat the words the priest gives me in unison with my brother, watching Xanthe as tears prick her eyes and roll down her cheeks. Her happiness is a glow that only deepens her beauty, and as she says the words back to me and Kiera echoes them, I'm filled with such unending love that I feel like my heart will burst.

As we kiss our brides, the room erupts with cheers and white rose petals descend from somewhere in the rafters above. The sheer happiness and joy are broken by a cell phone ringing, and Corbett, embarrassed, rushes down the dais and out of the room to take the call, followed by laughter from everyone.

Adam and I nod to one another and sweep our brides away into a dance on the dais. Within moments, the crowd is dancing in whatever opening they can find on the throne room floor, the happiness in the room contagious. Servants in emblazoned livery appear from nowhere and collect the chairs, clearing the room to be an open dance floor.

As I twirl Xanthe around, her curls fly loose and free, she's the epitome of magnificence. Beside us Adam and Kiera dance while holding hands with little Ginny. I say a silent prayer that our child will soon be announced as I turn Xanthe in a twirl and stop her with my chest to her back, my hands on her stomach.

"You see them?" I whisper in her ear, and she nods. "This time next year we'll be dancing with our own child," I promise her, and she leans her head back against my shoulder for a kiss.

"I can't wait," she breathes, her eyes overflowing with joy and anticipation.

Suddenly, the door bursts open and Corbett runs in.

"Brec, it's Mara, she's crashing."

CHAPTER 15
XANTHE

As we rush to the hospital, still in our fine clothes, I tell Adam everything. How I used to be a doctor and couldn't handle watching the children die anymore. How I found out about my cancer and I pushed my brother, my only surviving relative, away. I tell him how I couldn't leave the children, especially Mara, to die alone so I took the job on the security team. I'd been Mara's doctor for years, looked after her when her parents died in an accident, and I'd taken custody of her legally, leaving her everything I owned in the world should she survive me.

All the money I'd saved being a doctor had dwindled to nothing to pay for her care, and now she was dying anyway. I sob into my hands as I finish telling the tragic story. Adam and Kiera look at me with sympathy and little Ginny reaches out and holds my hand.

As we arrive at the hospital, Brec helps me out with a sad smile and the halls clear for us as we walk through. When we arrive at Mara's room I can hear her struggling to breathe, the machines are going nuts, the doctors and nurses scrambling. Doug is outside the door with tears streaming down his face.

"I knew you'd come," he says, taking in my appearance with confusion and awe. "Corbett paid for the new treatment, and I watched over her and kept him in the loop. He's a genius scientist, you know..." he mutters as I smile at him and squeeze his hand and enter the room.

Mara is lying in the bed, frail and pale, her eyelids almost translucent and her lips practically bloodless.

"Leave us," I demand, and all the nurses and doctors freeze. "She's suffered long enough." My voice cracks as I sit on the edge of her bed and take her hand in mine.

Mara's eyes are open and full of fear as she gasps for breath and looks around the room wildly. "My angel... My vampire..." she gasps as Brec sits on her other side and holds her other hand. "I don't wanna die, I want my mommy..." she cries, and I pull her up into my arms and hold her as her tiny body fails her.

"Can our blood do anything?" I beg, looking from Brec to Adam and Corbett as I sob openly. They all look away, saddened and defeated.

Corbett's shoulders sag. "I tried, Xanthe. My blood was the treatment, but for some reason, it didn't work. It worsened her condition."

A new wave of tears floods my face. I clutch the tiny girl, child of my heart, and sob as I feel her fading away. Her weak hands can't even squeeze me back, her tiny voice is too weak to speak.

"Can I meet her?" Ginny asks from her mother's arms and I nod, letting Mara lean back in my arms. Kiera sets Ginny on the bed and she crawls on her knees to look over my shoulder. "She's so pretty, auntie," Ginny says, stroking Mara's bald head. "You love her a whole bunch, don't you?"

All I can do is nod, trembling as Ginny smiles.

"She's like my daughter..." I tell Ginny, and she nods as if everything makes sense.

She slips around me, running a tender arm down Mara's skinny arm, then weaves their fingers together. I smile at her in thanks, glad Mara will be surrounded by love in these final moments, but Ginny raises the arm to her mouth. And bites Mara's wrist.

Gasps of shock echo from everyone in the room as I try desperately to get Ginny off of Mara, but I'm not strong enough and no one in the room can move Ginny an inch. Her eyes are closed, her face calm, as she sucks without apology.

I watch in horror as the remaining vestiges of color fade from Mara, leaving her whiter than the sheets. She looks at me one last time and cries, "Mama."

Mara goes limp in my arms and I wail at the ceiling, hearing the sound echo back to me. It's a sound I've heard in the children's ward many times, but I never thought I'd ever make it myself. The sound of a mother watching her child die. There's a sharp pain in my wrist, and a strong, tiny hand forces my bleeding wrist to Mara's mouth. The thick red blood drips past her lips, and my disbelieving eyes watch as Mara's throat works as she swallows.

Shocked into silence, I watch in utter wonder as Mara's skin turns pink. It starts at her mouth, flowing through her face and down her extremities. Black hair pricks the skin of her head and grows wildly, crazy curls just like mine. Her body fills out, her face grows plump like Ginny's, and I look up at her in disbelief.

"I just knew that would work!" she declares, bouncing on the bed and clapping. "I couldn't just let my cousin die, auntie, why are you so surprised?"

I look at Brec, Adam, Corbett. They're all as dumbfounded as me.

"Never in the history of our race has a human been successfully changed without being a Forever Bound mate..." Corbett whispers in awe, staring at Ginny with a newfound understanding. "The offspring of a Forever Bound couple has always been amazingly strong. Adam, a brutal fighter undefeated, but this, this is unknown territory." Corbett looks at Kiera. "Your brother might be capable of this, born of your mother and Thaddeus."

Everyone goes quiet as the implications set in. If the Monroes ever find out about this ability, the danger will be insurmountable.

I only have eyes for Mara, who suddenly shifts in my arms and curls up. Her eyes flutter open, full of so much life and love. My heart breaks with happiness. "Mama?" she says, sitting up and looking around the room. "I feel...funny."

I laugh a little, Mara has only known pain for her entire life. Struggling to breathe and constantly tired from her internal battle. Now her lungs aren't needed, her body strong and capable.

Ginny grabs her hand. "Hi, Mara! I'm your cousin, Ginny! We're gonna be the best of friends!"

Sitting next to the pool on Brec's lap, I smile as I watch the girls playing. Coming here to the chateau in Switzerland was the right decision. Brec and I took Mara here to keep her a secret, and Adam and Kiera joined us. The two girls have both grown so much in the few months we've been here, now looking to be about thirteen. Their bond has been unbreakable, and Ginny says Mara looks like me because I gave her my blood. Making her my daughter for real.

Brec wraps his arms around me, cradling the baby bump that's just popped out enough to be obvious. In the house I hear

Kiera barking orders, redesigning everything just like she did with Brec's apartment. No one dares oppose her, not only is she a formidable fighter, but she's always right with her design choices.

I turn my head, watching my new brothers and their father converse on the edge of the balcony. Corbett is talking about the assassin, how he's close on her trail and it won't be long before he catches her. Devion rolls his eyes at him, reminding him that it's more important to find another woman, his mate. Especially after seeing the sheer power that the bond creates. Zarius nods, silently agreeing, while Ever shifts on his feet, wanting nothing more than to play with the girls in the pool.

Ever may be full grown, but he's only two hundred years old, still a child in vampire years. I smile and wave at him to join them, and he jumps in the pool fully clothed. My father-in-law raises a brow at me and I smirk, making a gust of wind blow his crown off and down the chasm below the chateau. Devion and Corbett break out in laughter as Devion climbs over the balcony and informs his father he'll fetch it.

"Take me to bed, lover..." I whisper in Brec's ear and nip his neck, drawing a little line of blood and licking it off hungrily.

He stands up too fast, too eager, and almost drops me on the ground. Mara points and laughs at us but Ever splashes her and she completely forgets us and chases after him.

Brec takes me up the stairs running, stopping every now and then to kiss me passionately against a wall, and by the time we get to our room we're completely naked and ready. He sets me down on the bed and turns to lock the door. Outside the sun is setting and the floor to ceiling windows let in a gorgeous orange glow.

I stretch, basking in the light and rubbing the small baby bump with love and awe. Brec turns back to me, a wildcat ready to devour his prey, and kneels on the floor by the bed. He grabs my hips and pulls me to him with a growl, burying his face in the curls between my legs and giving me one solid lick as he watches me squirm in the light of the sunset.

In the past few months together, Brec has discovered everything about sex and what I like and dislike and now he prides himself in his professionalism. "You want to watch the sunset, my love?" he asks between my thighs, the vibration making me go nuts.

All I can do is nod and moan, and in a flash I'm on my hands and knees while he eats me from behind. Brec slides a thumb into my ass as he licks me thoroughly, his nose rubbing the entrance to my body and making me crazy. He licks around my folds, torturing me, only letting the slightest of touches land on my sensitive clit.

Growling, I grind my ass against his face and he laughs. "Watch the sunset, lover," he moans into me, and I almost lose my balance and fall onto the bed.

"I want you in me when I come..." I say breathily, and he makes an agreeing sound as he closes his mouth around my clit and sucks.

I arch my back, he knows this is the finishing move and he does it oh so well. His tongue swirls around the apex of my clit, soft and gentle, as he bites just hard enough to pierce the skin and flood his mouth with my blood and juices. I'm moaning wildly now, bucking his face so hard he has to hold my hips to keep me where he wants me.

He's such an expert that he can tell by taste alone when I'm about to come, and as the sensation overtakes me, he plunges inside my pussy. The orgasm is so intense, so fulfilling, that my arms go limp and I fall on the bed, biting the blankets and screaming my pleasure. Brec holds me up by the hips, fucking me slowly and deeply, hitting every erogenous spot inside me like he has a map of my body memorized.

I'm still riding the waves of the intense orgasm when he pulls me up, cupping my stomach and biting my neck. We watch the sun disappear behind the Swiss alps as he reaches his orgasm, filling me so thoroughly that if I wasn't pregnant already, I would be now.

Finally, we fall in a tangle of limbs on the bed, stroking each other and staring into each other's eyes as the world goes dark around us.

"Get a room!" Ginny laughs outside the door.

"Yeah! That's soooo gross!" Mara chimes, and they both run away laughing.

"Hey? Has anyone seen Mara? They're hiding from me!" Ever shouts as he runs past our room, too.

Brec and I burst into laughter, listening to the sounds of the house and our family at peace.

Ready for the next installment in the Forever Bound series?
Check out Chosen Blood!

CHOSEN BLOOD

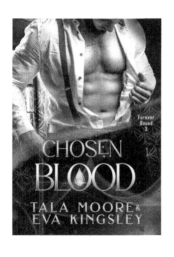

A Forever Bound is simply a matter of fated bloodlines. Someone who will strengthen the Cadell empire. An arrangement that can be reduced to some careful calculations.

And I know exactly who mine is.

Except the one who falls into my trap isn't the product of my algorithms. Dominique is a vampire hunter. Feisty and fierce, she's here for my blood.

And I refuse to taste hers. No matter how much it calls to me.

I don't care that we're stuck in this trap of my own making until the week is up. My fated mate for all eternity can't be a vampire hunter. Dominique can't be the one who will fortify the Cadell line.

My Forever Bound can't be the one who wants me dead.

Different worlds collide and enemies can't help but become lovers in this unforgettable paranormal romance. Corbett and Dominique's story is a steamy, standalone romance with a HEA that will leave you smiling and satisfied.

GRAB YOUR COPY HERE

https://mybook.to/ChosenBlood

FREE READ!

She cursed him as a punishment. It's a gift that changed everything.

He killed my friend, a goat I raised from birth, and for that, he shall pay. If the barbarian wants to act like a savage wolf, then he will live as one.

Except it's a King I've bound to my side. A furious one.

Nevertheless, Cassius is the enemy. He's rough and arrogant. Little did I know that underneath he's also honorable and protective.

His primal power is one I cannot deny.

Now we're trapped by a war I've always loathed, running for our lives, fighting growing feelings that neither of us understand.

Forces want Cassius' kingdom. But he now wants me, the witch who cursed him. I should say no. I want to say no.

But I can't.

The spicy prequel to the Apex Pack Series. For fans of a strong heroine who's not afraid to wield her magic and the powerful King who will show her even that is no match for love. A steamy, standalone paranormal romance powerful enough to create the first werewolf.

FREE WHEN YOU SUBSCRIBE TO OUR NEWSLETTER!
https://dl.bookfunnel.com/xk2ljalgj8

ALSO BY TALA MOORE AND EVA KINGSLEY

Another epic fated mates series co-authored by Tala and Eva!

APEX PACK

Find Me Tracker

Save Me Enemy

Mark Me Rogue

Match Me Wolf

Show Me How

Claim Me Alpha

Tie Me Down

Keep Me Safe

Catch Me Hunter

Heal Me Mate

Make Me Whole

TALA MOORE

SILVER MOON ALPHA

BLACK DIAMOND ALPHA

WILD HEART ALPHA

EVA KINGSLEY

EMILY'S GAME

About the Authors

Tala Moore loves all things paranormal and romance. Give her possessive alpha males, sassy heroines, and a love that refuses to be denied, and she's set for as long as she can disappear from the world (which is never as long as she'd like!). Learn more about her books at www.talamoore.com

Eva Kingsley is a dark paranormal romance author who dives into your darkest desires and deepest fears. She's not afraid to describe the macabre and and still give a memorable and passionate (if not obsessive) love story. Connect with Eva on Facebook.

Printed in Great Britain
by Amazon